Love Captive

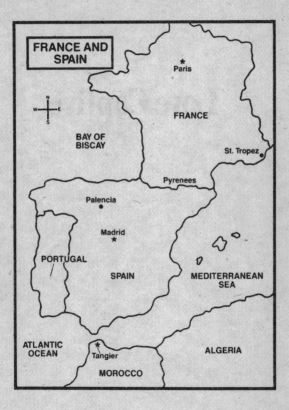

FRANCE AND
SPAIN

N
W E
S

Paris ★

FRANCE

BAY OF
BISCAY

St. Tropez ●

Pyrenees

Palencia ●

Madrid ★

PORTUGAL

SPAIN

MEDITERRANEAN
SEA

ATLANTIC
OCEAN

Tangier ★

ALGERIA

MOROCCO

"Just Who Do You Think You Are?" Anne Demanded.

Carlos's black eyes glared furiously into hers. "You've just told me who I am," he said, his breath coming hard and fast. "Your captor. Your enemy."

The next moment, Carlos stepped even closer, pulled Anne against him; and his mouth came down on hers, more demanding than ever before. Carlos's arms went around her and he held her pressed tight against him, his mouth capturing hers, possessing hers. Anne found herself almost unable to breathe. Her heart beat so fast it frightened her. She wanted to cry out, to break free, but she couldn't. Instead, she found herself responding to him, to the dizzying passion of his kiss.

JACQUELINE HOPE,
a Californian by birth, has been a housewife and a writer ever since her marriage in 1959. "Love and writing seem to go together for me," says the author, who has published numerous contemporary romances and is currently involved in writing soap operas and historicals as well.

Dear Reader:

During the last year, many of you have written to Silhouette telling us what you like best about Silhouette Romances and, more recently, about Silhouette Special Editions. You've also told us what else you'd like to read from Silhouette. With your comments and suggestions in mind, we've developed SILHOUETTE DESIRE.

SILHOUETTE DESIREs will be on sale this June, and each month we'll bring you four new DESIREs written by some of your favorite authors—Stephanie James, Diana Palmer, Rita Clay, Suzanne Stevens and many more.

SILHOUETTE DESIREs may not be for everyone, but they are for those readers who want a more sensual, provocative romance. The heroines are slightly older—women who are actively invloved in their careers and the world around them. If you want to experience all the excitement, passion and joy of falling in love, then SILHOUETTE DESIRE is for you.

I'd appreciate any thoughts you'd like to share with us on new SILHOUETTE DESIRE, and I invite you to write to us at the address below:

Karen Solem
Editor-in-Chief
Silhouette Books
P.O. Box 769
New York, N.Y. 10019

JACQUELINE HOPE
Love Captive

Silhouette *Romance*

Published by Silhouette Books New York

America's Publisher of Contemporary Romance

SILHOUETTE BOOKS, a Simon & Schuster Division of
GULF & WESTERN CORPORATION
1230 Avenue of the Americas, New York, N.Y. 10020

ISBN: 0-671-57145-1

First Silhouette Books printing April, 1982

10 9 8 7 6 5 4 3 2 1

Map by Tony Ferrara

America's Publisher of Contemporary Romance

Printed in the U.S.A.

Chapter One

As Anne McCullough glanced around the dimly lit, crowded nightclub, she noticed the tall, dark-haired man who stood toward the rear of the bar. At first glance she thought him the most attractive man she'd ever seen, with an aristocratic face so handsome it took her breath away. She wondered momentarily, excitedly, if he could be the man her brother Michael had sent her here to meet. The next moment she dismissed this possibility as wishful thinking. Still—in this small room swarming with dark-eyed, dark-skinned Arabs, only half a dozen men looked European.

Narrowing her eyes, Anne stared even more intently across at the man. Michael had sent her here to meet a man named Carlos Philip Alvarado-Castellon who, according to Michael, came from a wealthy Spanish family that had blood or marital ties to every royal house of Europe; Carlos himself would one day be a duke. The tall, slender man upon whom she gazed so intently was not only incredibly handsome, there was also something so self-assured about the way he stood, with such an arrogant tilt to his head, she could easily believe that through his veins coursed the blood of kings.

As Anne thought this, she felt her pulse pound hard with excitement. The next moment, laughing at herself, she forced her eyes to move away. Only in the movies did people look as they were supposed to look. In real life, appearances were almost always deceptive. The tall, arrogant stranger with the elegant air was probably the son of a cab driver and a hardworking seamstress. Carlos Philip Alvarado-Castellon, heir to a dukedom, would most likely turn out to be a hefty, swarthy-complexioned man who looked like a small-town butcher. Smiling at the thought, Anne swung her eyes back around to enjoy the sight of the attractive man standing by the bar.

Her attention focused across the room, she was unaware that she was receiving a number of interested looks herself. The light-brown hair shot with gold, and pale blue eyes which had always seemed so ordinary back home were attracting fascinated stares here in this land of dark-eyed, dark-haired beauties. More than one interested male had caught sight of the slim, fair girl in the navy-blue traveling suit who sat all alone at the corner table. Anne, who had chosen the suit for the efficient, businesslike air it lent her, was totally oblivious to the fact that it also emphasized the feminine curves of her figure and brought out the blonde highlights in her hair. Absentmindedly sweeping the golden curtain away from her face, Anne smiled to herself.

It still seemed impossible to her that she was here, in a crowded little nightclub in a rundown section of the city of Tangier, Morocco. Two days before she'd been safely home in Baltimore, Maryland, secure in her dull little rut. Then Michael had phoned, pleading with her to drop everything to fly to Morocco to help him. He had written and phoned her before about his hectic romance with Dorrie—Dolores Camilla Marie Matilda Alvarado-Castellon. They'd met in Venice, Italy, when both were there as tourists, had found each other enormously interesting and attractive, and Dorrie had repeatedly sneaked away from the aunt who was acting as her chaperone to spend time with Michael. When the aunt caught on, she had angrily dragged Dorrie home to Spain, to her father's castle in Palencia. Dorrie's passport had been destroyed, she had been stripped of all funds, and kept under virtual house arrest. For several weeks a frantic Michael hadn't heard from her, then she'd written him to meet her in Salamanca; she was going to run away and meet him there. Once they'd been reunited in Salamanca, they'd fled south to Algeciras, and there had hired a local fisherman to take them across the narrow straits to Tangier, Morocco, with Dorrie's brother Carlos in furious pursuit.

Now they were holed up somewhere here in Tangier—even Anne didn't know where—hoping to get a passport for Dorrie so that they could fly home to the United States to be married. Carlos had left word all over the city that he wished to meet with Michael to discuss the situation, and Michael had agreed to meet him here. But then, at the last minute, instead of keeping the rendezvous himself, Michael had asked Anne to go in his stead. She had long been planning a vacation from her rather routine banking job in Baltimore and this seemed the perfect excuse to get away. She had time off coming to her, and money saved up in the bank. So—as impossible as it all seemed—here she was.

As Anne continued to eye the man standing across the room, she saw the bartender lean across the bar to speak to him. The man glanced around to look at her, his handsome face impassive. He offered the bartender a slight solemn bow, then began walking toward her, making his way easily through the crowd to where she sat.

He came to a stop on the far side of her tiny table. "Excuse me, miss," he addressed her in clear, unaccented but curiously uninflected English, "I am told you are the one I have come here to meet. I am Carlos Philip Maximilian Alvarado-Castellon, at your service. May I sit down?"

"Why, of course, please do," Anne said quickly, the words tumbling out. Excitement made her head spin. As Carlos drew out the chair and seated himself across the small table from her, she tried hard to calm herself, in particular to kill off the silly grin of pleasure she could feel spreading across ler face. To be thrown into the company of such an incredibly handsome, elegant, self-assured man—

"So—how are you enjoying your stay in Morocco?" Carlos addressed her. His black eyes, under slashing dark brows, gazed steadily across at her. Anne felt her breath catch again. Close up, Carlos was even more handsome than she had thought him before. He had an arrogant, refined face, with an aquiline nose, a surprisingly sensuous mouth.

Thick, straight black hair and flashing black eyes marked him as a true son of Spain. If this was what royalty looked like, no wonder the common man had bowed down, for so many centuries, to pay homage to the aristocracy!

"Well, I—I really haven't had much chance even to get my bearings yet," Anne responded, still feeling breathless. A quick, joyful smile spread irresistibly across her mouth. "I arrived only a few hours ago, at four this afternoon."

"After a smooth and uneventful flight, I hope?" Carlos remarked, the corners of his finely molded mouth curling into a very slight, perfunctory smile in answer to hers.

"Oh, yes, a very nice flight," Anne agreed. If only she could catch her breath properly, calm the excited pounding of her pulse, and concentrate on the real purpose of this meeting. Any minute now, she knew, Carlos would drop these pleasantries and—and then what?

Before saying anything more, Carlos glanced away. He sat for a moment gazing idly around the room, a look of distaste spreading across his face. Anne glanced around too, seeing with dismay what she knew Carlos was seeing—the inappropriateness of the meeting place her brother had chosen. The small room they were in was dreadfully crowded, with postage-stamp-size tables all but jammed against each other. Behind a small dance floor four musicians sat playing instruments that Anne couldn't identify. The music they played sounded strange and grating, a harsh screeching in her ears. The air was thick with smoke, the noise level nearly deafening. Possibly—hopefully—Carlos would suggest that they leave here and go somewhere else.

His dark eyes circled back. "What word is it that you Americans use for a place like this—a dive, is it? This is a dive, yes?" He paused, his black eyes gazing even more intently at her, and then he said, "And why is it your brother allows you to come to a dive like this? Has he no more respect for you than that?"

Anne's pulse leaped uncomfortably. "It isn't a question of respect," she answered hastily. "He . . . just felt that an out-of-the-way place like this, in a . . . less affluent part of town, would be safer, that's all."

"Safer?" Carlos echoed the word, looking genuinely puzzled. A small smile flickered momentarily across his mouth. Glancing around, he said, "Surely no place could be less safe than this. Never would I allow my sister to go alone to this part of the city, believe me." His smile dying away, he set his lips in a firm, disapproving line as he once again glanced back at her.

Anne felt a small twitch of amusement curl her mouth. "Oh, I believe you—" she almost addressed him as "Carlos," then caught herself; possibly that wouldn't show sufficient respect this early in their acquaintance. "But—if I may say so—this is surely one of the differences between your culture and ours. Between how things are considered and done in the Old World, that is in Spain, and in the New World, at least in the United States. Back home, my brother has no right to say one way or another whether I go to a club like this. He is not my guardian or chaperone any more than I am his. I am a free adult, my own person, and I don't need Michael's permission for anything I do."

Carlos eyed her even more intently, if possible. "Ah, yes," he said, "but your brother didn't just 'allow' you to come here, he sent you here. Surely even in America that makes a difference. I would not send even my worst enemy, if she were female, to a place like this."

Anne felt more than a touch of annoyance. "And neither would my brother," she answered rather tartly, "under other circumstances. But I've already explained to you he felt that a club like this would be . . . well, that we'd run less of a risk in a place like this. He is dreadfully concerned that if and when he meets you, as he has agreed to do, you will have him followed and in this way will learn where your sister is."

"And that is what you meant by safer!" he exclaimed softly, a slight smile tugging on his mouth. "Ah, you Americans," he added a moment later, "how you love your intrigue, yes? Please excuse my saying so, but possibly your brother has seen too many movies. For this reason, we must meet in this foul-smelling, filthy club, and when I arrive here, instead of seeing your brother, as I expected to, I am met by a woman. And not even one with whom I might hopefully converse on a somewhat meaningful level. Rather than sending, as envoy, his father, an older brother, or even his mother, whom does he send? A snippet of a girl, even younger and less responsible than he is!"

As Carlos glanced arrogantly across with a long-suffering, condescending look, Anne felt her earlier annoyance slip into anger.

"I am not a *snippet*," she snapped, "nor am I younger than Michael, or in any way irresponsible. The fact is, my brother is twenty-two; I am twenty-four. We don't have an older brother to send, and our parents are dead. And I'd like to know exactly why you can't deal with me?"

"You're twenty-four, you say?" Carlos responded. "Believe me, you don't look it. I took you for about sixteen."

This was said in a tone so close to contempt that Anne felt anything but flattered. Her anger deepened into such rage she could feel the blood pounding through her veins. "Well, whether I look it or not," she cried in fury, "I do happen to be twenty-four, and I don't care who you are, Carlos Philip Whatever, you will either start speaking to me with respect or this meeting is over right now! Do you read me, mister?"

"If you mean, can I hear you," Carlos answered, his voice suddenly even softer, "not only can *I* hear you, half the other people in this room can hear you, despite the cacophonous wailing of those four musicians. Is it your desire to create a public scene?" He leaned slightly toward her over the table while saying this, his black eyes spitting contempt at her.

Anne leaned over toward him, lowering her voice, whispering shrilly back, "No, it is not my desire to do that, nor to have anything at all to do with you, believe me. But I came here as my brother's envoy—"

14

"Because he was too frightened to come here himself," Carlos interrupted, "after agreeing that he would do so."

"Because he knew he couldn't trust you!" Anne almost shouted in her fury, drawing back again. "And now I can see why. Now, are we going to work toward having a reasonable discussion or shall I leave?" She pushed her chair back an inch, ready to rise if her arrogant companion uttered one more contemptuous word.

Instead of making any move to stop her, Carlos leaned back in his chair. Black eyes still flashing contempt at her, he airily waved her off. "Go ahead, leave. That's all I would expect from you, considering who you are, sister to that fortune hunter. But, let me warn you, I shall find a way to reclaim my sister despite you both."

Half standing, Anne wavered. She bit her lip nervously, then allowed her blue eyes to move down to where she was looking directly at Carlos again. At the sight of his magnetically compelling gaze, her anger seemed to drain out of her and she felt breathless again, and rather weak. With a small, dismayed smile, she sank back onto her chair.

"Look, Carlos," she said, the first time she had dared to call him that, "we've obviously gotten off to a very bad start, so let's begin all over, all right? I'm Anne McCullough," she ended, extending her hand across the table to him as her lips moved into a friendly smile.

In a surprisingly quick and graceful movement, Carlos shot to his feet. He took her hand in his as he smiled in answer. "How do you do, Anne McCullough? It is my pleasure to meet you. Is it all right if I sit down?"

"Of course, please do."

Anne smiled even more broadly, in relief and pleasure, as Carlos reseated himself. His black eyes gazed steadily across at her, his slow smile giving that aristocratic face a new warmth and undeniable charm.

"You are right, Anne McCullough," he said, "we did get off to a bad beginning, for which I apologize. I had hoped very much to see your brother here and—"

"I know, and I'm sorry," Anne murmured placatingly. "When he explained the situation to me, I honestly tried to get him to come here with me, as he'd agreed to do, but Dorrie—"

"You refer to my sister Dolores?" Carlos interrupted, with a slightly startled look.

"Yes, your sister Dolores. Michael kept calling her Dorrie, so that's how I think of her. Anyway, he said Dorrie heatedly objected to his having agreed to meet you, that she kept insisting—and I hope you won't take offense at this—but, anyway, your sister insisted that you were not to be trusted. She said that you were so intent on getting her to return home with you that there was nothing you wouldn't stoop to to achieve that. So in the end Michael gave in to Dorrie's tears and decided to send me here in his place."

Carlos listened to this explanation with his head slightly tilted, an intent expression on his face. "Ah, I see," he murmured when Anne finished. "And my

16

sister is right, of course. I will do anything within my power to locate her and take her home. That's why I am here, in Morocco. But what else would any family do when a young girl has been kidnapped?"

Anne smiled. She almost gave in to an impulse to reach over to touch her companion's hand, but at the last moment she restrained herself.

"Oh, come on, Carlos," she said almost teasingly, "you know perfectly well no one kidnapped your sister. She met my brother, they fell in love, and, knowing your family would never approve of their marriage, they ran away together."

"Fell in love?" Carlos echoed grimly, drawing back, his black eyes once again glowing coals. "She's twenty years old, a child, what does she know of love? And most certainly she is right that our family will never approve of her marriage to this man. If only I could see her and talk to her, I know I could bring her to her senses and persuade her to return home with me." '

Anne felt a fresh wave of annoyance. How coldly sure of himself Carlos was, how insufferably arrogant! "Well, I haven't yet had the pleasure of meeting your sister," she responded rather haughtily, "but from what Michael said, she's deeply in love with him and determined to marry him no matter what your family says or does. Their plan is to fly to America as soon as possible and get married there, where the custom is for people to marry because they're in love, as Michael and Dorrie are."

"And where a third of your marriages end in divorce!" Carlos shot at her with a sneer. "That's what comes of marrying for what you Americans call love! Marry today, divorce tomorrow—that's the custom, is it not? What does my sister know of this Michael except that apparently he pleases her senses? What do they have in common, tell me that? On what can they base a marriage? On the pleasures of the senses? Ah, yes! Fall in love today, get married. Fall out of love tomorrow, no matter, get a divorce. You may accept that as a pattern of living for your brother, but I reject it for my sister. The next time you see your brother just tell him that: I reject this so-called love they share, I reject his plans for my sister's future, I reject him! If he were half a man he'd meet me so I could tell him face to face!"

Carlos drew back in his chair, sitting stiffly upright, his black eyes flashingly alive in his otherwise controlled face. Anne stared across at him feeling oddly moved and deeply upset. Was Carlos right? *Would* Dorrie be better off if she forgot about Michael and returned home? When Dorrie and Michael came from such disparate backgrounds, had so very little in common— Oh, dear, Anne thought, and became aware that her head now hurt, as well as her heart.

Blinking, she swung her eyes from Carlos and glanced out across the crowded nightclub. The blue-black smoke in the air seemed even thicker, and the wailing music more discordant. Tangier, city of mystery, city of intrigue, a city where East met West, where Africa and Europe mingled. And tonight, Anne thought wryly, unhappily, a place where New World romantic independence met Old World arrogant nobility. And from this meeting would result—God only knew.

"So?" Carlos interrupted her thoughts a moment later. "You suggested a reasonable discussion—about what, if I may ask? What more is there for us to say? I wish to meet with your brother, to try to talk sensibly with him. He agrees to meet me, then sends you instead. Where do we go from here, as you Americans so picturesquely put it?"

Carlos once again looked directly across at her. His proud face looked, it seemed to Anne, just a slight bit tired. She felt a shiver of fatigue—and pleasure—run down her spine.

"I don't know, Carlos, you tell me. At the moment I'm feeling dreadfully tired, far too tired to think. I've gotten practically no sleep since Michael phoned me two days ago. I've spent endless hours flying halfway around the globe. And so far, this hasn't turned out to be much of a vacation. At the moment I am suffering not only from near exhaustion but also from jet lag, not to mention a great uneasiness at finding myself in a city that I find very strange. So don't expect me to come up with any startling or brilliant suggestions, please."

As Anne's words died away, she flashed out a quick, nervous smile. To her great pleasure, Carlos smiled back, his sensuous lips curving lazily into that wonderfully attractive smile.

Leaning forward he said, in a quiet, friendly voice, "I know what you mean about being tired. I'm dreadfully fatigued too. Since Dolores ran away four days ago, I've scarcely slept. Believe me, I am as anxious as you to bring this whole problem to some resolution, no matter what it turns out to be. If only I could see your brother and talk to him, I'm sure we could come to some agreement. If I can't talk sense into him, possibly he can convince me of the strength of his position. Then I could return home to convince our father, and Dolores could come out of hiding, obtain a proper passport, and fly to America to be married, yes? Why does your brother so stupidly refuse to meet me?"

As he spoke, Carlos leaned even farther forward. This brought him so close that Anne found it hard to breathe. His black eyes, no longer flashing contempt, seemed suddenly very deep, surprisingly intimate. Anne felt pleasurable shivers run through her. Besides being so incredibly handsome, surely Carlos was right. If Michael believed in what he was doing, if he believed that he and Dorrie had a right to be together and to marry, then he should talk with Dorrie's brother. It was stupid and cowardly not to do so.

"Have you a telephone number for him?" Carlos asked in the same confidential tone. "Surely you do. Why don't you go phone him right now and tell him I'm here, still hoping to meet him? No matter how long it takes for him to get here, I'll be happy to wait. And you needn't fear I'm trying to trap you. I'll sit right here at this table, in open view, while you go to the bar to use the phone. How can this possibly hurt your brother? Please, Anne, will you phone him?"

It was the first time he'd called her by her first name alone. Anne felt her heart jump wildly. Carlos was right, he was only asking her to do what was sensible. But still . . . no, he was right. Michael should agree to come.

"All right," she said decisively. "I do have his number and I will go phone him. Excuse me, please."

As she rose, Anne was aware she was trembling, but exerting all the control she could gather, she turned from the table and made her way through the crowd to the bar. When she asked the bartender for the use of his phone, pantomiming dialing a number, he grinned quickly at her, motioned her to the end of the bar, and placed a dial phone before her.

As she picked up the receiver, Anne knew a moment of doubt. Was Carlos tricking her? She glanced around to see if he was keeping his word, if he was still seated at their table, but the crowd blocked her view. She bit her lip, took a deep breath, and began to dial.

Michael answered, on the fourth ring, in a voice that sounded high and cautious. "Hello?"

"Michael, it's me, Anne. I'm still here at the club where you sent me, and Carlos is here too. Michael, he's terribly upset that you didn't come yourself, as you'd agreed to do, and he wants very much to meet you. He says he'll wait here for you for as long as it takes you to get here. Won't you come?"

After a marked hesitation, Michael said, "Wait a sec." He was gone for what seemed a very long time. When he picked up the phone again, he said, "Can you hear that, sis? Dorrie's crying and screaming at me, she's so upset at the mere suggestion, so there's no way I'll go there. Dorrie knows her brother and she says he's sure to have two or three hired thugs there with orders to follow me home when I leave. We'll have to think of some alternate plan."

21

Eight minutes later, the call completed, Anne returned to the table. Her cheeks warming in embarrassment, she repeated to Carlos what her brother had said.

"But he told me of another place where he's willing to meet you," Anne said slowly, her head now hurting even more; she couldn't remember ever feeling so dreadfully tired. "He says if you want to drive to . . . to Tay's boat, he'll meet you there. Do you know where that is?"

Carlos's face had tightened as he listened. When Anne finished, he gave a curt nod. "Yes, I know where that is. Come along, let's go." He shot gracefully to his feet and quickly stepped around the table to take Anne's arm to help her up.

"You . . . want me to go along?" Anne asked, startled by Carlos's sudden movement.

"Of course I want you to come along," Carlos shot back, in a cold, formal voice. "I had a drink before you arrived, so I'll have to stop by the bar to pay for that, and then we'll leave." His hand clutching her arm, he pulled her through the swarming crowd, his touch as cold and formal as his voice. What had happened to the warm intimacy with which he had persuaded her to call her brother?

He did trick me, after all, Anne thought, and she felt a deep, deep sadness sprout in her heart.

Chapter Two

Carlos grabbed her arm again as they left the club. He guided her down the dark sidewalk toward a small car parked at the curb. Just as she climbed into the car, Anne felt, rather than saw, some movement in the shadows. Glancing quickly around, she caught sight of a small, thin man scurrying away down the walk. Swinging completely around on the seat, she peered into the darkness behind the car but couldn't really make anything out. Still she knew. The pounding of her heart told her. And made her furious.

Carlos climbed in behind the wheel, started the motor, pulled out from the curb. He kept his eyes straight ahead and did not speak.

"So—your sister was right!" Anne spat at him in fury, staring at his handsome profile with rage and contempt. "You did have a hired hood all staked out to follow Michael home if he came here to meet you. You don't really want to meet with him to talk to him at all, all you want is the chance to track him down and corner your sister!"

"Hood?" Carlos echoed. He glanced around at her as he flashed out a hard, amused smile. "And

23

what is this 'hood'? Oh, wait, wait, never mind, I know. American gangster slang, yes? Hood, an abbreviation of hoodlum. And I hired a hood, you say?"

"You know perfectly well you did, at least one, maybe more." Anne swung angrily around to peer through the tiny back window. A car followed them less than half a block behind, headlights gleaming through the dark. "When we came out from the club, you must have motioned for him, or them, to follow, and that's what they're doing." She swung back around, glared at Carlos a moment, then snapped in fury, "Stop this car right away and let me out, please."

"What?" He sounded genuinely startled, even a touch worried, as his dark eyes swung around.

"You heard me!" Anne felt a sweet surge of triumph. "Stop this car and let me out. You're using me to lure my brother into a trap and I won't let you do it. If you don't stop right now, I'll open the door and throw myself out, I swear I will." Taking hold of the door handle, Anne, breathing hard, tried to gather her nerve to make good on her threat.

With a worried expression, Carlos reached across, grabbed her hand, and pulled her away from the door. "Now calm down and behave yourself," he ordered grimly. "That car you said was following us—look back again. Where is it now?"

Swinging her head around, Anne again stared through the tiny rearview window. Behind them the road was dark, there were no headlights anywhere in view. Swinging forward again, she felt both weak with relief and more than a little embarrassed.

24

"All right, it looks as though I was wrong. And if I was, I apologize."

"Apology accepted." Carlos laughed briefly, then threw her a friendly smile. "You, like your brother, have seen too many movies, I think. You Americans, how you dramatize, how you love to make a big, splashy production out of everything. And how you like to characterize others as cold, insensitive brutes, while you yourselves are above reproach. If one couldn't laugh about it, one would be forced to weep."

As Carlos's deep, soft voice died away, a mask seemed to fall over his face. Again he looked straight ahead as he drove and said nothing more. Staring at him, Anne felt a hunger stir within her, a need to have those black eyes glancing at her again, even if they spat contempt. The new silence that hung heavy between them was almost more than she could bear.

Still Carlos continued to look straight ahead and did not speak.

In time, sighing, Anne drew her own eyes away. She rested her head back and closed her eyes. The moment she did, the image of Carlos leapt into life behind her closed lids, his proud bearing, his handsome, aristocratic features, the seemingly bottomless black eyes intently fixed on her. Sighing again, she reopened her eyes.

"Exactly where is it that we're going?" she asked, too tired to really care but hungry to hear his voice, hoping to start a conversation.

But all Carlos said in response was, "You'll see," and again he fell silent. His narrow, long-fingered hands held the wheel firmly yet without apparent strain. Even sitting casually as he was now, there was something unnervingly commanding about his bearing, about the way he held his head. He wore dark slacks, black loafers, a dark green turtleneck sweater. He is *so* incredibly handsome, Anne thought, and again forced herself to rest her head back and to close her eyes. Carlos Philip Maximilian Alvarado-Castellon, who was completely out of her reach, who would one day be a duke.

The movement of the car lulled her, and before very long Anne drifted off into sleep. She had no real idea how long they'd driven when the car slowed, then stopped. As Anne jerked upright, blinking, she saw Carlos turn to her with a smile.

"We're here now, my tired little friend." There was a hint of amused tenderness in his voice that immediately set Anne's pulses to racing. As his dark eyes held hers, he leaned toward her. For one electrifying moment Anne could only think that he meant to kiss her. Instead he leaned past her to throw open the door.

As he drew back, he smiled. "You asked me to stop the car so you could climb out; now I have and you can." He smiled even more broadly, then turned away to climb out of the car.

Shaking her head a bit to wake herself up, Anne climbed out too. It was so dark that for a moment, as she stood peering around, she could make nothing out. She felt relieved and happy as Carlos stepped up beside her.

"It's very dark here, is it not? But this is where your brother directed us to come. If you'll wait a moment, I'll fetch a light."

As he walked away, Anne almost cried out to him to stop, not to leave her there all alone in the dark. But, biting her lip, she held the cry back. She could hear Carlos's steps moving away, then she heard nothing. Gradually her eyes adjusted to the blackness, and peering ahead, Anne thought that possibly she could see the outline of a boat. Then she could definitely make out a swinging light, and soon Carlos was back at her side, holding a lantern that threw off a soft, flickering light.

"Come along, Anne." Carlos took her arm and guided her forward. "We're parked near the pier where Tay's boat is moored. Now, step up here onto the pier." He held the lantern low so Anne could see where to step. They began walking along the dark pier side by side and soon Anne could clearly make out a boat.

"It's a small cabin cruiser," Carlos informed her, "belonging to a man Dolores and I have known all our lives, Tay Dominquez. If this is where your brother wishes to meet and talk with me, so be it."

As Carlos fell silent again, Anne could hear the lapping of the water against the pier. Even as the sound calmed and soothed her, it excited her too. Suddenly she could think of nothing more poignantly romantic than to be right here where she was, with an incredibly handsome Spanish nobleman at her side, in Tangier, Morocco. Suddenly Anne grinned to herself, remembering what Carlos had said in the car. If he had the least notion of what she was thinking about at this moment, he would surely burst out laughing. Then he would probably lecture her on how Americans, seeing far too many movies, were not only painfully melodramatic but hopelessly romantic as well. And . . . he'd be right.

When they reached the boat, Carlos climbed aboard first, then hung the lantern on a pole and turned back to help her on. As she stepped aboard, he momentarily held her by both arms, smiling down at her.

"All we need is a full moon, and this is the perfect setting for romance, no?" His black eyes intently fixed on her, he started to lean down to kiss her. Before he had done so, however, a shadow crossed his face and he drew back again. "But possibly you have no romantic notions about a man like me—one who does not believe in true love," he remarked, and his hands dropped from holding her arms.

Swinging away, again taking the lantern, he started down the side of the boat, motioning for her to follow. They traversed a narrow passageway until they reached some stairs. After they'd descended the stairs, Carlos clicked on a light and led Anne into a small cabin.

Glancing around, Anne noticed that the cabin was beautifully appointed, with warm polished wood almost everywhere. There were double-decker beds against one wall, a closet, a half-open door leading into a washroom. In the center of the room there was a small table with four chairs. Carlos motioned her to one of the chairs.

"Are you hungry? This isn't my boat, as I've mentioned, but there's surely food in the galley with which I can make us a snack. Or a cup of coffee perhaps?"

"I'd love some coffee, thank you," Anne murmured, still feeling wistfully sad over the kiss that they had almost shared.

Excusing himself, Carlos left the cabin. Anne went into the washroom. She worked to repair her makeup and combed her straight, shoulder-length hair until it shone. She stepped back into the cabin just as Carlos returned holding a mug of steaming coffee in each hand.

Without speaking, he placed the two mugs down on the table and seated himself. Again Anne watched in fascination at how elegantly graceful his movements were. He picked up his mug in both hands, blew off steam, and began to sip. "Ah, just right," he murmured with a quick little smile. "Hot and strong. I hope that's how you like it too."

"Yes, thank you, I do." Anne seated herself across from him and, picking up her mug in both hands, began to sip too. Over the rim of her mug she looked directly at Carlos. His dark eyes circled up to meet her pale blue ones. They sat for several moments looking intently at each other, then, frowning, Carlos lowered his eyes and his mug.

"You're a very pretty girl, Anne McCullough, a real American beauty. I suppose that means that your brother is a remarkably handsome man. And my foolish young sister, delighted with your brother's appearance, can't distinguish between physical infatuation and proper affection, which stems from a common background and heritage. And on this superficial, fleeting feeling of physical attraction, she stupidly thinks she can build a marriage."

"Which lots of people manage to do!" Anne replied heatedly, stung by Carlos's words. "Some

American marriages end in divorce, I grant you that, but that doesn't mean that most of them do. And for two people to marry for any reason other than love is—is exploitative and opportunistic!"

"Well, well," Carlos answered, flipping out a coolly contemptuous smile. "Those are strong words. Exploitative and opportunistic, you say? If I had a fortune-hunting scoundrel of a brother, I don't believe I'd use those words quite so glibly and freely. The one way my sister Dolores can protect herself from being exploited, from being married for her name and fortune, is by marrying a man whose position and fortune are equal to hers. If anyone is an opportunist, it is your brother, not I."

Anne blinked against sudden hot tears. She knew she had been bested in the exchange, but still she couldn't resist continuing the argument. "You just absolutely refuse to believe that the two of them fell sincerely in love, don't you? You just won't admit that that's what happened. That my brother Michael might be, and is, a wonderful young man fully deserving of your sister's love, and that Dorrie, far from being duped, knows exactly what she wants and what she is doing. That possibility absolutely escapes you, doesn't it?"

Carlos eyed her steadily with a scornful little smile. "Yes, I admit that that possibility strikes me as completely absurd." He stood up, black eyes arrogantly fixed on her pale face. "As completely absurd, in fact, as any notion that you and I, for instance—well, you see what I mean." He turned and left the cabin, leaving her to struggle with even more pressing tears.

Oh, I hate him! Anne thought first, furiously grabbing up a tissue from her purse to wipe her eyes. Oh, but isn't he right? she thought next. Or . . . is he right? He was so handsome, so incredibly dynamic. He was also a wealthy man, heir to a title. He would one day be a duke, the woman he married a duchess. How much of the sharp hunger she felt for him now was based on what he was as a person—did she really have the least idea what he was like as a person?—and how much on what she knew about his family background and money? Had he turned out to be the son of a cab driver and a seamstress, as she'd speculated there in the bar, would she have the same intense, painful interest in him now?

Trying to be as honest with herself as she could, Anne admitted that quite possibly she wouldn't. But—if that was the case, how did a man like Carlos protect himself from being exploited, from being chased by greedy, scheming women? By sticking to those in his own special sphere, of course. By socializing with those who had the same wealthy background he had. Which was precisely the point he'd made.

Yes, he's right; unfortunately, he's right, Anne decided, wiping away the last of her tears. He and I don't belong together, and quite possibly Michael and Dorrie don't either. After all, American marriages, based as they so often were on little other than a strong physical attraction, did end in divorce a heartbreakingly high number of times. Therefore, Carlos had every right to do as he was doing, to try to persuade his sister to return home and avoid what could very likely prove to be an extremely costly

31

mistake. *Okay, Carlos, you win,* Anne thought wearily, *you win.*

She had regained complete control of herself by the time Carlos reentered the cabin, carrying a tray with two plates of sandwiches.

"I decided I was hungry after all," he announced in a coolly distant voice, "so I went to have a look and found the makings for tuna fish sandwiches. I made one for you too, if you want it. If not, no matter." He placed their plates on the table and slid the tray to the floor. Reseating himself without looking at her, he picked up his sandwich.

After a moment, sighing, Anne decided that she too was hungry. With a murmured, "Thank you," she began to eat.

They munched away in an unfriendly silence, Anne doing her best to forget her companion's presence. She felt a sharp sadness well up in her, and suddenly found herself remembering times when, as a small child walking by her mother's side through large department stores, she had been told sternly that she could look but not touch. She smiled wryly to herself, realizing she felt that same hungry yearning now that she'd felt then, the need to touch and stroke and hold in her arms the marvelous things she saw. But . . . she couldn't then and she couldn't now. She'd been born into a poor family, and when they'd gone shopping, her mother had always been fearful that her children might damage expensive merchandise for which she'd be forced to pay. There had never been enough money to buy her the things she craved as a child, and now that she was grown, nothing had changed. She was still too poor and nameless to ever have for her own the man for whom her heart now ached. But for Pete's sake, Anne scolded herself, choking down the sandwich Carlos had fixed for her, I've only just met him, and if there's one thing that's certain it's that I'll most certainly get over him.

Over him? Anne's thoughts echoed, and she heard herself burst out laughing. How tired she must be to be taking herself so seriously! How could she possibly think that what she felt for Carlos was anything but the silliest kind of schoolgirlish infatuation? So he was handsome, rich, a Spanish nobleman—so what? The fact remained that she'd met him only a couple of hours before and knew next to nothing about him. To imagine herself falling in love with him . . . Still laughing, Anne raised her eyes and looked directly across the table, genuinely amused at herself.

"What's the joke?" Carlos asked curiously, black eyes lifting to meet her gaze.

"Oh, nothing." Anne sipped from her mug. Putting the mug down, she added casually, "I was just thinking about what you said, you know, about how you and I— Suddenly I could see what you meant, how utterly ridiculous such a pairing would be, and I found myself laughing about it, that's all. I didn't mean to offend you."

"Most certainly you haven't offended me," Carlos responded coldly, sounding offended nonetheless. "As you said—as I said earlier—it is of course a completely ridiculous notion. That is not to say that I don't find you attractive. You're an extremely pretty girl, as I acknowledged earlier. Naturally any healthy male, as I consider myself to be, is going to . . . well, physically respond to you. That's only normal, how could it be otherwise? And to find myself alone with you like this, late at night on a gently swaying boat . . . But tell me, do you not feel it, too? Do you sense this same attraction between us?" His voice was low and seductive as he leaned over to take her chin in his hand, forcing her eyes to meet his ebony black ones.

"I . . . I . . . don't know," she stammered, lost in the velvet depths of his gaze. She did not understand what had come over her. Only a minute before she had been laughing at the impossibility of anything between them. Yet now—why was her heart hammering so? Why did she find herself longing for the touch of his lips? It was impossible, he'd said so himself. "If only you weren't who you are," she murmured, more to herself than to him.

"Yes, if I weren't who I am," Carlos echoed in a soft, faraway voice; then abruptly he took hold of Anne by both arms and drew her up. He pulled her against him, and his strong, sensuous mouth came down on hers. He kissed her very softly at first, then slowly his lips hardened and the kiss deepened. From the moment he'd touched her, all thought deserted Anne's mind. As he held her close she felt almost suffocated with excitement, with the need to press herself even closer to him, to melt against him and into him. But before she had lost control enough to do this, Carlos suddenly thrust her away again and released her arms.

"But I am who I am," he muttered. Without giving her a second glance, he turned and strode out.

Sinking down onto her chair, Anne stared after him, watching him disappear.

He was gone for what seemed a very long time. Anne sat at the table slowly sipping her coffee. At the sound of his steps returning at last, she rose and swung to face him. Carlos stopped just inside the door, frowning at her. His face looked even more grim, it seemed to Anne, and his eyes even blacker.

"I've been up on the pier," he explained, "swinging the lantern around as a welcoming signal to your brother, but there's no sign of him. What time did he say he'd meet us here?"

"Well, he—he didn't say," Anne stammered, startled by Carlos's question. She'd forgotten all about Michael, about the fact that Michael had said he'd come tonight to meet them, that that was their sole reason for being here. "But I—surely he'll get here anytime," she added weakly.

"Of course," Carlos snapped impatiently, "unless this entire trip was a—how do you put it?—wild-goose chase. Would this be your brother's idea of a joke, do you think, having me drive miles and miles out here for no reason at all? Or after agreeing to come, did he simply lose his nerve, too much of a coward to face me?" After contemptuously spitting out these words, Carlos spun on his heel and left again.

This time he was gone an even longer time, so long, in fact, that Anne considered following him out to see what he was doing. But—what would be the point of that? And where in the world was Michael? Oh, she was so tired, all but completely exhausted. At last, standing up, Anne gathered together the dirty dishes and left the cabin, finding her way to the small kitchen. She rinsed off the crockery, then set the dishes to dry. Yawning, half asleep on her feet, she returned to the cabin, used the washroom, then decided to lie down for a time on the lower bunk. This was the last thing she remembered. The moment she stretched out on the bunk and put her head down on the pillow, she must have fallen asleep. Her last thought was of Carlos. Aside from that she remembered nothing until she woke the next morning.

Chapter Three

So—Michael hadn't shown up after all.

This was Anne's first thought as she woke in the morning. She swung up to a sitting position, feeling ashamed for her brother, and, by extension, ashamed of herself.

As she walked toward the washroom, yawning, she wondered where Carlos was, and whether he was terribly angry.

As she emerged from the washroom, Carlos came striding in carrying a mug of coffee. His stern face, framed by the thick, gleaming black hair, was every bit as handsome as she'd remembered it. His black eyes not meeting hers, he handed the coffee mug to her.

"This will have to do for breakfast, then we're on our way. After a stupidly wasted night!" He spun on his heel and left the cabin.

Within a few minutes they were off the boat, walking down the short wooden pier to where Carlos's car was parked. Carlos strode silently at Anne's side, barely controlled fury on his face. As they hurried along, Anne glanced briefly over her shoulder, her attention caught by the bright blue water that stretched away in one direction toward the horizon.

"Carlos, I'm afraid I haven't the faintest idea where we are. I know Morocco borders both the Mediterranean Sea and the Atlantic Ocean, but which body of water is this?"

Momentarily Carlos ignored her, then he glanced contemptuously around, eyes spitting arrogant sparks. "You may not know your way around Morocco," he responded condescendingly, "but we're still on the planet earth, where the sun continues to rise every morning. It's about an hour after sunrise, so if you'd bother to look, you could figure out for yourself which body of water this is. I presume that you do know in which direction the sun rises."

As his ridiculing voice died away, Carlos's black eyes focused for a moment on Anne's face, then with a contemptuous smile he circled his eyes away again. Her cheeks flushing with embarrassment, Anne glanced into the sky for the sun. She located it low on the horizon to their left. They were walking south, she calculated, therefore it was not the Atlantic Ocean behind them but the Mediterranean Sea.

"Thank you, Carlos, for straightening me out," she murmured icily, "and for doing it so graciously."

"You're welcome," he snapped, and nothing more was said.

After they'd climbed into the car, however, Carlos swung to face her, black eyes blazing, and addressed her again.

"There's one message I wish you to give your brother for me," he remarked with cold fury. "Tell that fortune-hunting scoundrel that while *Dorrie* comes from a reasonably wealthy family, she herself is all but penniless—and if she goes through with her plans to marry him, she'll remain penniless, I can assure you. Father will immediately cut her out of his will and so shall I. The fortune our family has at the moment does not come from inherited wealth, but from the labors of my father and myself. Forty years ago, our father, who was educated as an engineer and happens to be a brilliant man, founded a company for marine engineering, which for the past few years I have run in his stead, and it is from this company—which has full control over various patents that my father and I have filed—that our present wealth comes. If it weren't for this, we'd be part of the impoverished nobility scattered all over Europe, people who can barely scrape together the wherewithal upon which to live. But if your brother is under the impression that he has won a girl who is wealthy in her own right, I—"

"Oh, I'm sure he doesn't think that," Anne interrupted furiously, "and wouldn't care in any case!"

Carlos's black eyes fastened on her, flashing righteous contempt. "And I'm just as sure he *does* care," he ground out, and lapsed into angry silence.

The same heavy silence lay between them all during the hour's drive back to Tangier. Anne tried to lift her depressed spirits by eyeing the unfamiliar countryside, but the effort didn't succeed. In time Carlos drew the little car up in front of the Grand Hotel Villa de France, as Anne had requested. He remained silent, staring straight ahead, as Anne reluctantly climbed out.

She stood by the open door a moment, undecided as to what to say. "Well—Carlos, I'm sorry about last night, sorry about everything," she murmured at last. When he still didn't speak, simply nodded imperiously to indicate he had heard, she felt she had no choice but to close the car door and let him leave.

Though Anne had been at the Grand Hotel briefly the afternoon before, just long enough to check in and leave her baggage in her room, she hadn't paid much attention to her surroundings. This morning she forced herself to glance around. The hotel, set in a luxuriant garden, was really quite impressive. As she entered the lobby and walked across it, Anne was even more impressed by the interior, which was superbly appointed with Moroccan-style decor. But as hard as she tried to be pleased with her surroundings, they did little to lift her spirits. Why hadn't Michael come to the boat last night after agreeing that he would?

In her room Anne took a long, soothing bath, put on a fresh white linen dress, and managed to get an outside line on her telephone. She dialed her brother's number.

"Michael? Michael, what happened? Why didn't you come last night after you said you would?" Tears of anger—of fatigue—of depression, flooded into Anne's blue eyes.

"Now, hold on a minute, sis," Michael said in a low tense voice. "I did come—but I'll explain it when I see you. Are you alone now? Are you back at the hotel? Good. Go downstairs, catch a cab to the Solazur Hotel, Avenue des F.A.R., which is right on the beach, and I'll meet you in the lobby. See you there."

In twenty minutes Anne climbed out of her cab at the Solazur Hotel and when she entered the lobby Michael came striding up to meet her. With an affectionate grin, he pulled her close for a brotherly hug. His sandy hair flopping boyishly down on his brow, he drew back again to stand and smile at her.

"Anne, I appreciate what you're doing for me. I can't tell you how much. Let's go walk on the beach."

As they strolled along the white sandy beach a few minutes later, Michael kept peering behind them to make sure they weren't being followed. Anne, reminded of Carlos's comment that Americans, having seen too many movies, dramatized everything, was beginning to find it annoying. Wasn't Carlos right? At this particular moment she felt far too hungry, tired, and depressed to appreciate the veil of mystery that Michael was throwing over everything, and she honestly doubted the need for it. If only she could forget this whole stupid business and begin enjoying her vacation!

"All right, Michael, why didn't you show up last night?" she demanded to know.

Michael's light green eyes met hers. "Not now, Anne, please. I did come—but I'll explain it all to you in just a few minutes. Let's duck back to the street and catch a cab."

"But—but I thought we were already near where you live, within walking distance!" she snapped in exasperation.

"Hardly!" Michael responded, laughing. His attractive young face glowed with health in the early morning light. *He's enjoying this, all this dramatic nonsense!* Anne thought, and more than ever she agreed with Carlos. Michael, and possibly Dorrie too, had simply seen too many adventure movies, and now they were delightedly creating a phony adventure for themselves. If they'd just meet with Carlos, sit down and talk reasonably with him, surely some sensible resolution could be reached.

They soon managed to hire another cab which took them through narrow streets lined by closely crowded, whitewashed structures. In about twelve minutes, Michael motioned to the cab driver to pull over. He paid the driver, jumped out of the cab, and pulled Anne out.

"We're living right around the corner from here. Dorrie has a room toward the back, while I'm sleeping in one at the front of the boarding house. We've told our landlady we're brother and sister, here on vacation. She's a deaf old woman who doesn't seem to pay much attention to anything. Here, here we are."

Michael glanced carefully up and down the street, then hurriedly pushed open a heavy, whitewashed door and motioned Anne in. She stepped into a narrow, dim hallway. Michael followed her in, closed the door, and led her off down the hall.

He stopped before an open door. Frowning, Michael stepped through it, pulling Anne in after him. "Dorrie? Dorrie, where are you?"

Scowling, Michael dropped Anne's arm and stepped away. Glancing around, Anne found she was in a small room with white walls and a brightly woven carpet on the floor. A narrow cot was placed along the front wall. Strung across the room were various ropes, with drying wash slung over the lines. Michael ducked under the nearest line, momentarily disappearing from view. A moment later he reappeared at Anne's side, his green eyes nearly frantic.

"She doesn't seem to be here. You don't suppose—"

At that moment soft steps came into the room. As Anne swung around, she saw a lovely, fair-skinned, black-haired young woman who bore a strong family resemblance to the man from whom she had parted only two hours before.

"Oh, thank God, here you are!" Michael exclaimed. He rushed over to close the door behind the girl. "For God's sake, Dorrie, don't scare me like that. When I saw you weren't here, I almost had a heart attack."

"Silly." The girl smiled lovingly at Michael. She reached up to press a kiss on his cheek. A moment later she stepped over to Anne, extending her hand. "Hi. I'm Dorrie, and you must be Anne. I'm so delighted to meet you. You know, of course, that I'm madly in love with this brother of yours!"

Dorrie's dark eyes danced. She put her arm through Michael's and drew him up close beside her. "My family, of course, objects strenuously, but I won't give Michael up and no one can make me. I love him dearly and he loves me and we're going to be married, no matter what!" Dorrie's sparkling black eyes looked adoringly up at Michael, while his attractive young face beamed down at her.

Anne found herself both touched and annoyed by this pretty picture of young love. "Yes, yes, I know," she responded with a touch of tartness. "But why must it be done this way? I was with your brother Carlos last evening, you know, and he is terribly anxious to meet Michael and talk with him. Surely you can't expect your family to approve your marrying a man they have never even met? Yet though Michael agreed to come, and set up the place of meeting himself, still he failed to show up."

"Anne, I *did* come, I swear it," Michael responded with an answering touch of tartness. "Just ask Dorrie. I left here right after your call, hired a cab, and headed out to where the boat was moored. But I've had sufficient experience with dear brother Carlos, and I've listened to Dorrie carefully enough, that I also took precautions to make sure I wasn't being led straight into a trap. And believe me, sis, last night I was."

In exasperation, Anne snapped, "Oh, come on, Michael, you were not. You're just making a big cops and robbers thing out of this when it needn't be that way at all. For a time I too thought that Carlos and I were being followed, but I learned I was wrong. There were only two of us on that boat last night waiting for you, Carlos and I. And that's the truth."

"On the boat, yes," Michael agreed, his expression now serious. "But as we approached the pier, I had the cab driver shut off his lights. We passed the pier, swung back around, and then I had him suddenly switch his lights back on—and you know what we saw? Both of us saw it. Two men crouched

44

under the pier, enjoying a smoke, waiting for me to walk along the pier so they could rush out and jump me. Somehow, in spite of all our precautions, Carlos was able to arrange it. So I had the cab driver speed up and get me out of there."

As Anne stood staring at her brother, her head spun. She couldn't quite believe him, yet how could she not believe? "But—but why would Carlos want to do that?" she sputtered at last.

Dorrie threw her head back and laughed. Stepping forward, she took hold of Anne's arm with her small, soft hands. "Oh, you naïve Americans! You and Michael too, you are both so naïve. You just don't understand a man like my brother—a clever, devious man like that—he's quite beyond your experience. Dear sweet Anne, don't you understand even yet? My brother is bitterly opposed to this marriage and will stop at nothing to find me and drag me home. So what if it means assaulting Michael and kidnapping him?"

Anne's startled blue eyes flew from Dorrie's face to her brother's. "And you—you think that's what those two men were there for?"

"Of course I do," Michael snapped impatiently. "Carlos figures that if he could grab me, and keep me locked up somewhere for a week or so, that would force Dorrie out of hiding and he could grab her too. The man will stop at nothing, don't you understand?"

Dorrie ran her arm through Anne's and led her forward, under the lines of drying wash, toward the cot by the wall. Smiling, she pulled Anne down to sit on the cot.

"But please don't look so unhappy," Dorrie pleaded softly, looking upset herself at Anne's distress. "It's not that my brother is really a monster; he just can't help being the way he is. Don't you see, from the day he was born he was taught to rule, constantly reminded of his responsibilities and aristocratic duties. Our mother, before she died—God rest her soul—worshipped the ground he walked on. He is accustomed to power, to giving orders and having them obeyed . . . instantly."

Dorrie paused, a soft smile spreading across her well-formed mouth, a mouth—Anne thought as she stared at it—so like her brother's that last night had kissed her.

Dorrie smiled sadly. "Now you must see, Anne, that he loves me very much. He feels that as my older brother, it is his duty to care for me. Carlos expects me to marry a man my family knows and approves of. He does not believe in love at first sight. . . ."

"Is he married?" Anne interrupted suddenly, not knowing she was going to ask any such thing. She bit her lip nervously, self-consciously, wishing she could draw the question back.

"Married?" Dorrie echoed sadly, with the same soft smile. "No, dear Anne, he is not. I know that on occasion he has been—how shall I say it?—romantically involved with women he considers inferior to him, but he would never think of marrying such a woman. Someday he will, of course, marry some dull, bloodless woman he considers his social equal, and they will live together in their dull, bloodless marriage without a hint of happiness or passion, while I"— Dorrie's dark eyes danced and she jumped up suddenly and wound her arm possessively through Michael's—"while I shall be deliriously happy with my even-tempered, considerate, sweet, sweet Michael! When one thinks of it that way, one has to feel sorry for poor Carlos, no?"

"No," Michael muttered, but he grinned down at Dorrie as she smiled up at him.

Suddenly Dorrie giggled, a delightfully schoolgirlish sound. "And the crazy thing is, dear Anne," she said, leaning down toward Anne with an impish sparkle in her clear black eyes, "the thing that Carlos is so proud about, our family—what is there to be so proud of, I ask you? Are we not people just like anyone else at heart?"

Dorrie laughed again, a rich, amused laugh, and Anne found herself smiling in response. But as her smile died away, she felt a sudden sharp pain in her heart. If Carlos was in truth the person that Dorrie had just described—but of course he was. She had seen enough of him to be certain the description was accurate.

Michael suggested they stop wasting time and begin making plans. When she'd run away from home, Dorrie had had sufficient presence of mind to bring with her some jewelry that was hers. "My mother left it to me," Dorrie explained. "It was to be mine the day I got married, and now I'm getting married, right?" The day before, Michael had met a man who claimed to have connections in Casablanca. This "connection" would happily furnish them with a forged passport for Dorrie in exchange for a piece of jewelry. "Then off we shall fly to America," Dorrie said, "to live happily ever after, yes?" Her eyes shone with joy.

"Now here's what we want you to do," Michael told Anne. "Go back to your hotel, check out, catch a cab to the airport. At the airport, exchange the ticket you have for one going out of Casablanca, going home by way of Paris. Once you've made that exchange, rent a car and come back here. Dorrie and I will be ready to go and together we'll drive down to Casablanca. That way, if Carlos is still tailing you, he'll be sidetracked to Paris, while we will be left in peace to get Dorrie's passport."

"All right," Anne agreed.

In an hour and a half she was back, her rented car pulling up in front of the small, whitewashed boarding house where Dorrie and Michael waited. The front door opened and out they came, Michael carrying two suitcases, Dorrie one. Between them they managed to get all the cases stashed into the trunk. Michael offered to drive. Dorrie sat in front beside him while Anne sat in back.

"'So we're off on the road to Morocco,'" Dorrie sang happily, and Michael joined in. Anne listened to them, smiling wryly to herself. What an exciting, amusing, splendid adventure they were weaving for themselves, and surely everything would work out all right as it always did in lighthearted, romantic movies. The villainous, black-hearted brother Carlos would be thwarted, and— Aware of a sudden sharp pain in her heart, Anne closed her eyes.

The day passed in a long, weary haze. The paved road along the coast down to the city of Rabat, though sometimes quite narrow, was easily traveled. Anne occasionally entertained herself gazing out at the gently rolling green hills; at other times she enjoyed the sight of the Atlantic Ocean. In Rabat they stopped to eat, going to a restaurant on the beach, the Caravelle, which served French food. After a pleasant meal, they were off again on the broad paved road from Rabat to Casablanca, a sixty-mile stretch which Anne drove, with Michael and Dorrie in back.

Somewhat to her surprise, Anne found, when they arrived in Casablanca, that it was a clean, shining, modern city, with wide streets and tall modern buildings. Somehow it made her feel even more homesick and she couldn't wait for this nonsensical trip to come to an end so she could fly home.

At midnight they drove to the airport. Finally it was time to bid Michael and his sweet, smiling Dorrie good-bye. Michael gave her final instructions about her stay in Paris. He gave her the name of a small, inexpensive *pension* where he had stayed when in the city. He would phone her there in two days, by which time, hopefully, everything would be settled and they would know for sure that they didn't need her anymore. Meanwhile, he insisted, she should relax and enjoy her stay in the most enchanting city in the world.

"You'll love it there, Anne, believe me," Michael told her, kissing her cheek in farewell. "And thank you so much again for everything. Take care, sis."

After Dorrie had kissed her too, Anne turned at last and walked onto her plane, deeply relieved to be leaving. In the mood she was in she might not love

Paris, as Michael forecast, but it was bound to be an improvement on Tangier. And in two days—hopefully—she'd be free to fly home to her beloved Baltimore.

She settled down in her seat, closed her eyes, and tried to sleep.

Sleepless hours later, she dragged herself and her one case wearily off the plane at Orly Airport near Paris. Suddenly she felt her heart nearly stop. A tall, black-haired man stood watching the disembarking passengers. *Carlos.* So Michael had been right!

His watching eye caught sight of her and remained focused on her. Feeling instantly furious, Anne walked over to face him. Obviously, Michael and Dorrie understood him far better than she—Carlos *had* been following her movements, just as they'd predicted, and he'd fallen right into their trap! She was disgusted with herself for having halfway believed in him despite her brother's warnings.

"Well—Carlos. How in the world did you get here?"

His sensuous lips moved into a small, cold smile. "Easily enough. A dear friend was kind enough to fly me here on his private jet."

"Ah, of course. But—how did you know I'd be on this plane?"

Carlos's cold smile broadened a bit. "To trace the movements of an attractive, brown-haired, blue-eyed American girl in a North African country is not all that difficult," he explained.

"Ah, of course," Anne said again. "But—next and final question, I hope: *Why* are you here?"

Carlos didn't answer at once. He grabbed up

50

Anne's case, took hold of her arm, and began leading her out of the airport. "Because, my dear Anne McCullough," he said finally, "I am tired of playing this cat-and-mouse game with your lying scoundrel of a brother, and I've learned of a new development that means I no longer have to. When I phoned home yesterday morning after I left you off at your hotel in Tangier, I learned from my aunt that your brother not only abducted my impressionable young sister, he also stole thousands of dollars' worth of jewelry, some of the pieces priceless heirlooms that have been in our family for centuries. So—don't you see?—I no longer have to pursue him myself, all I have to do is go to the police and have them issue a warrant charging him with grand theft. Simple, yes?"

As Anne stared in shock, she felt her knees almost give. "But—but Dorrie took that jewelry, which she says belongs to her. Michael didn't steal it—how could he have? He was never in your home, he and Dorrie met in Salamanca. How do you dare claim he stole anything?"

Carlos gazed scornfully at her out of cold, black eyes. "That may very well be," he murmured. "However, point one, though much of the jewelry will one day belong to my sister, when she marries with our father's approval, it is not hers yet. Point two, surely it is only a technicality that your brother was possibly not right there on the scene. Do you imagine that when I report this theft to the police, they will pin me down on unimportant details like that?" Smiling, Carlos shook his head as though saddened by the incredulity of this naïve American girl. "Ah, no,

51

there will be no problem, I assure you. If the case should ever reach court, your brother might be able to clear himself. Who knows? I seek merely to have him found and arrested, not thrown into prison. Shall we proceed?"

As Carlos again led her forward, Anne felt weak with shock. Despair threatened to overwhelm her; she'd never in her life felt so powerless. Then Carlos turned to her once more.

"However," he said, "our family has always shunned publicity and loathed having our name appear in the public press. Even in a situation as serious as this, we still instinctively recoil from being in the public eye. So when your brother phones you, as we both know he will, I wish you to give him this message: I will refrain from reporting any of this to the police, on one condition—that as long as he has physical custody of my sister, I shall have physical custody of his. If you both agree to this, you and I will drive together to my home. There your brother will join us, returning my sister unharmed, and unwed, to us. At that point I shall return his sister to him, also unharmed and unwed. If you don't agree—" Carlos gazed steadily at her with a cold little smile.

I'm going to faint, Anne thought, as her knees started to give. "Then—then what you're saying—?"

"Is that you and I shall drive together to my home in Palencia, Spain," Carlos repeated rather impatiently. "It's either that, or the police. For as long as my sister remains your brother's prisoner, you shall be mine. It's as simple as that."

52

Carlos began leading Anne forward again, his fingers angrily clutching her arm. Oh no, Anne thought, still feeling faint. Carlos and herself—their immediate futures now welded together quite as closely as Michael's and Dorrie's. Unless—unless, of course, she could think of some way out.

Chapter Four

As they walked toward a line of waiting cabs, Carlos asked, in a reasonably friendly voice, "Where are you staying?"

Anne felt her pulse give a frightened leap. "Give me a minute to think, please." She drew her arm free of Carlos's hold and stepped nervously out of the path of the crowd leaving the airport.

With a look of disdain, Carlos followed. His well-shaped mouth moved into a small, scornful smile. "Surely you know where you plan to stay, so what is the point of this childish delaying tactic?"

Her pulse racing, Anne tried to consider the situation, to see whether there wasn't some way out. She was *so* tired, so ill equipped at the moment to deal with this stupid mess. Should she admit to Carlos where she planned to stay, or would that simply be playing into his hands? Was it possible that he was only bluffing, that he hadn't the least real intention of going to the police with his utterly false charge? Oh, why had Michael dragged her into this ridiculous affair in the first place? All she wanted was to walk back into the airport, buy a ticket, and return home!

With her pulse suddenly racing even faster, Anne reached what she told herself was a firm decision. Her eyes circled around to challenge the arrogant man impatiently waiting at her side.

"Carlos," she said, "I've decided that I've had all I want of this stupid cops and robbers business. Michael was never in your home and could not possibly have had anything to do with your sister's taking the jewelry, which in any case she claims belongs to her. Therefore I'm not going to cave in under your threats and be blackmailed into going anywhere with you." Anne took a deep breath, then added in an even firmer voice, "What I am going to do is walk right back into the airport, buy a ticket on the first available flight, and return home. The three of you may resolve this mess any way you like, but from now on count me out."

An amused glitter sprang to life in Carlos's black eyes. "Fine." He again took hold of her arm. "I'll walk you back in, and to prove there are no hard feelings, I'll even remain long enough to make sure you have no problem making your wishes known, though possibly you are so proficient in French you need no help from me or anyone. *Vous parlez français, non?*"

As Carlos swung her around and courteously led her back inside, Anne felt her heart sink. She had absolutely no intention of trying to fly home tonight, but Carlos had called her bluff. No matter how angry she might be with Michael at the moment, she couldn't desert him, especially without even letting him know of Carlos's threat.

Anne stopped walking and faced her companion.

"All right, Carlos, you win. I don't plan to leave for home just yet, not until there's some resolution of this whole stupid mess. But I'm feeling so dreadfully tired; I do wish we could get it all settled as quickly as possible."

Carlos flashed her a warm smile, tucking her hand over his arm in a far more friendly fashion. "That is my wish, too, Anne, believe me. And you know how we might get it settled very quickly, within a few hours? Phone your brother and tell him what I've told you, that I plan to go immediately to the police if he does not return my sister. Once he hears this and realizes that I mean it, he will surely see that the jig is up, as you Americans so quaintly put it. If he were to put Dolores on a plane for Paris immediately, then this entire problem could be resolved within a very few hours. What do you say, Anne?" Carlos's dark eyes gleamed with what seemed to be friendliness as they gazed steadily at Anne.

Oh, no, no, you don't! Anne thought instantly in response to that look. *That's just the way you looked at me in that sleazy little bar in Tangier, and then you led me straight into a trap when I fell for it. Not again, mister. You can just save your phony smile, that charm you turn on and off like a spigot, for someone else. I'm wise to you now.*

"That would be just peachy keen," Anne countered tartly, "except for one or two minor things. Your sister does not happen to have a valid passport at the moment, thanks to you and your father, and—"

"But by now she surely has obtained a forged one," Carlos interrupted, flashing Anne a warm, charming smile. "That was the purpose of your driving them down to Casablanca, am I not right? So if you'll stop making up excuses, please, we'll make faster progress toward the goal we both so avidly desire."

With anger suddenly spurting through her, Anne stopped walking. She yanked her arm free of Carlos's hold and glared furiously at him. "Kindly cut that out, Carlos. Stop acting as though we're bosom buddies, united in our wish to achieve the same thing, because, believe me, we're not. You tricked me in Tangier and you're not going to do it again. For all your indignation and pretended innocence when I accused you of having us followed from that club, you had two of your men all set to pounce on Michael the moment he showed up at Tay's boat, though how you managed to arrange it—" Anne shook her head in puzzlement, still glaring furiously at Carlos, her breath coming hard.

The warm friendliness faded out of Carlos's eyes, replaced by a steely glint of arrogance. His lips moved apart in a cold, condescending smile. "Child's play, believe me. I told you I had ordered a drink from the bar, so when I went to pay for that—"

"You had already bribed the bartender!" Anne broke in indignantly. "So that was how!"

"*Bribed?*" Carlos's smile grew even icier, even more contemptuously condescending. "If you mean that I offered him a small amount of money for his cooperation, of course I did. That you should make that sound like something criminal—a bribe indeed! —merely shows once again how myopic you are about this entire situation. Ah, you self-righteous Americans! Your brother abducts my sister, you fly over to aid and abet him, yet in both your eyes *I* am the criminal. In dealing with people like you, why should I not seek alliance anywhere I can find it?"

Breathing so hard it was painful, Anne continued to glare in fury at this monstrously self-assured man whose eyes spit such lofty contempt at her. "So you told the bartender where we were going—"

"I did. I also arranged for two men to meet me there, to stay in concealment under the pier and take your brother into custody the moment he showed up. But he failed to show up, as both of us know." Carlos paused a moment, glancing impatiently away, then his eyes circled back. "But why are we dredging up this ancient history? That is over and done. You say I tricked you, yet I was the one who wasted an entire night with nothing to show for it. Now, however, the tables have turned, and I ask you: Will you phone your brother now or not?"

Anne stared angrily at Carlos a moment longer, then, as her eyes dropped, she felt a deep sigh rise within her. Though it hurt her to see it, it was time she faced the fact that Carlos was precisely the man his sister had said he was, obsessed with his own desires, unable to see that anyone else had any rights at all. If he could calmly hire two thugs to attack Michael, to take Michael into "custody," as he so self-righteously put it, then he would surely not hesitate to go to the police with a phony story about Michael's being guilty of theft. The situation was hopeless.

"Well, will you call or won't you?" Carlos demanded again, impatiently.

With a second, smaller sigh, Anne swung around and began walking again, out of the airport. Carlos fell immediately into step beside her.

"Carlos, quite possibly I would if I could," Anne remarked wearily. "But I haven't a way in the world of reaching him. I have to wait for him to phone me."

"And how soon will that be?"

Anne shrugged, weary tears edging into her eyes. "Two days, he said. He and Dolores didn't want me to return home until they were sure they wouldn't need me anymore. They were feeling so happy, so full of hope—" *And just wait until they hear what I now have to say!*

"Then you do know where you plan to stay, as I assumed you did," Carlos snapped with obvious anger. "Otherwise your brother wouldn't know where to phone you. You little fool! You say you're tired, and heaven knows I am too, I'm ready to drop. Yet still you play games. We could have been resting in a cab for minutes now, speeding toward our destination. When are you going to realize there is no way for you to beat me and that you might as well give in and cooperate? It would make everything so very much easier."

Sure—for you! Anne thought in fury, glancing sideways at the man for whom she now felt enormous contempt. But for the moment at least he seemed to be so firmly in control that to try to obstruct him anymore tonight seemed foolish even to her. More than anything else right now she needed a good night's sleep. Maybe in the morning —oh, surely in the morning everything would look brighter again. Maybe she'd even be able to think of some way out.

When Anne woke in the morning, she gazed around the room she found herself in with a confused, almost frightened feeling before she remembered where she was. *Paris*. The most romantic city in the world. Suddenly frowning, she lay in bed struggling to remember half-forgotten lines: *Oh, London is a man's town*—and then what?—*while Paris is a woman's town, with flowers in her hair.* Anne smiled softly to herself, enjoying the thought. Paris, with flowers in her hair. Except that somewhere in the city lurked Carlos, like a bumblebee ready to sting and paralyze her. With a deep sigh she climbed out of bed.

Michael wasn't due to phone until tomorrow, which meant that she had an entire day to herself, in Paris, the City of Enchantment, the City of Light. Washing and dressing, Anne made a firm decision: In spite of everything, Michael and his messy romance, Carlos and his arrogance, she was going to enjoy her one solitary day in Paris. She would push all worries out of her mind and simply let go and enjoy herself!

As she emerged onto the sidewalk from the small *pension* where she was staying, Anne saw with pleasure that it was a lovely day, warm and bright. Without any very clear idea of where she was going, she turned to her right and began walking briskly toward a nearby intersection. She had tried to communicate with the tiny, white-haired woman running the boardinghouse, but the woman did not understand English and, sadly enough, Anne understood only the most common French words. Any conversation in French more complicated than *"Bonjour, mademoiselle"* was quite beyond her. She had gotten the impression that possibly the tiny Frenchwoman had been offering her breakfast, but, not completely sure, she had merely smiled, bowed her head, and left.

She wasn't terribly hungry at the moment anyway, so she would simply walk until she ran across a café or restaurant. The fact that the only money she carried was U.S. currency, and that she would need to exchange her dollars for French francs before buying herself anything, had not yet crossed her mind. All her mental energy was engaged in the nearly impossible task of pushing out of her mind all thought of the future as she decisively insisted to herself that she was going to enjoy the day. Let go and enjoy. Live in the present. All her life she'd dreamed of someday going to Paris and now that she was here she was going to see all she possibly could, pack into her one free day here every delight imaginable. Paris. The City of Light, the City of Love.

"Anne! Over here, Anne!"

Anne became aware of the beep-beep of a horn at the same moment she heard her name called. Startled, she stopped walking and glanced around. A small car swerved into the curb and braked. From behind the wheel a tall, elegant figure emerged, waving imperiously to her over the top of the car. It couldn't be, but it was—Carlos!

"Climb in the car, Anne. It's illegal to park here, and the last thing I need is a ticket. Come on, get in." Carlos dropped down and disappeared inside the tiny car again. Anne caught a renewed glimpse of him as he leaned across the front seat and threw open the passenger door for her.

In an instant fury, Anne told herself that she wasn't going to do as he said. Why should she? This was her one and only free day, her one chance to see and enjoy the sights of Paris. Why should she allow him to spoil it for her? She owed him nothing, and at this point he could scarcely threaten her with anything more than he already had. Until Michael phoned her tomorrow and she could give him Carlos's message, Carlos would almost surely restrain himself and not rush angrily to the police, an action he had made it reasonably clear he did not want to resort to. So just let him buzz off, in his fancy little car!

Throwing her head back, Anne began walking briskly forward again, ignoring the little car that crept along the curb keeping pace with her, pretending she didn't hear the constant beep-beep of the horn. Anne reached the intersection, glanced about, and swung around the corner to the right. She was in a neighborhood of large old houses, many of which looked centuries old, and the sidewalk down which she hurried was so narrow two people could scarcely pass each other on it. The street seemed almost as narrow, as though two cars going in opposite directions might have some difficulty passing each other. No wonder so many European cars were compact or subcompact.

As she continued her fast pace down the sidewalk, Anne no longer heard the beep-beep-beeping horn. She glanced around and saw no sign of Carlos or his car. Thank goodness, he must have given up. Anne slowed her pace a bit, suddenly aware that she was famished. She hadn't the least idea where she was. The night before she'd given the *pension* address to Carlos, who had relayed it to the cab driver, and she'd been far too tired to pay any attention to the direction in which they'd gone. Not that it would have helped much had she paid attention. Anne glanced rather worriedly ahead. Where in the world was a café, or a bus stop? If only she could catch a bus into the heart of the city. . . .

At that thought, Anne felt her heart plunge down. Oh dear, how could she catch a bus when she hadn't a French sou on her? The first thing she'd have to do, before she could eat or go anywhere, was convert some of her American money into French. Abruptly she stopped walking, feeling suddenly overwhelmed by it all. Here she was, alone in a foreign city where she spoke scarcely a word of the language, not knowing where she was at the moment or where she wanted to go. What a beginning for a day she had resolutely determined to enjoy! That moment she felt an almost irresistible impulse to swing around and run back to the *pension*, where at least she had a room with a chair to sit on and a bed to weep on. With gestures, she might even get it through to the tiny little woman who ran the place that she was dreadfully hungry and would truly welcome some food.

As she stood debating her next move—whether she was going to give in to hunger and fear and return to the boardinghouse or stick by her resolution to see the city and forge courageously ahead—Anne felt a hand clamp down on her shoulder, hard. She was so startled and frightened she jumped. Her eyes jerked around.

"Oh, Carlos, it's you," she said, almost but not quite admitting to herself the relief she felt. "I thought you'd given up and gone away."

Carlos's well-shaped mouth moved into an arrogant little smile. "Proving how little you know me. Believe me, Anne, I never give up—on anything. My car, which I arranged to rent this morning, is parked in an alley a block away. Now why don't you be a good little girl and come along with me as you should?" Taking her arm, he attempted to swing her around.

Instantly irritated, Anne attempted to draw her arm free. "Who says I should? The Almighty Carlos? I wish you'd get over the notion that the entire world owes you obedience. I personally owe you nothing. I thought I had made it perfectly clear that I have absolutely no intention of going anywhere with you!"

By then Anne had managed to pull her arm out of his grasp and she stood glaring at Carlos. Oh, how this man infuriated her—and how incredibly handsome he looked in the clear morning light, with his aristocratic features and shining black hair! If only his beautiful form didn't house such a cold, scheming, unrepentant viper! Anne felt unexpected and fervently unwelcome tears come into her eyes. She felt suddenly so hungry and angry she was dizzy.

Carlos stood before her, his black eyes directly meeting her blue ones. His expression was one of controlled annoyance, as though he were a teacher about out of patience after repeated attempts to deal calmly with a difficult child.

"Look, Anne, I don't dare leave that car parked where it is very much longer. I came by your *pension* this morning to make sure you were still there. I wanted to make sure you hadn't pulled some trick and taken off during the night to fly back to Morocco." Carlos's lips curved in an almost friendly little smile. "Proving, I know, that I don't trust you, just as you showed clearly last night that you don't trust me. But you *are* still here, which I have to admit was a big relief, and here is my suggestion now. You say your brother plans to phone tomorrow, and you have no way of reaching him sooner. All right, I accept that. I will take your word for it, partly because I obviously have no choice. But if that is the case, we both have this day free, have we not? And I venture to suggest that you have never been to Paris before and would enjoy seeing some of the sights. Am I not right again? So here is my suggestion. Let us both put aside our distrust and dislike of one another and join forces for a day of enjoyment and sightseeing. What do you say?"

Anne squinted her eyes against the bright sun. "Well, I— Let me think about it a moment, all right?" Her pulse pounded hard.

Carlos broke into a soft, friendly laugh, again taking her arm. "What is there to think about? Possibly you'd rather go sightseeing on your own, but let us be practical about it. Have you any French money on you? By the time you get to a bank and make the exchange, half your day is gone. Even more important, are you sure you remember enough of your high school French to make yourself understood? Textbook French and French as it is spoken here are not always the same."

In spite of herself, Anne laughed too. By then Carlos, who held her arm, was leading her off down the sidewalk, meeting no resistance from her. "I'm afraid it's even worse than that," she admitted. "For some reason I can no longer remember, I chose to study German instead of French, so I don't even have a high school language course to fall back on. Truthfully, I was getting more than a little worried as to how I was going to get around."

Carlos glanced around to smile at her, black eyes twinkling. "So I shall be your guide and interpreter, right? And then someday, if we happen to find ourselves in Berlin, you can return the favor, *n'est-ce pas?*"

Anne laughed even harder. "Oh, of course. What I remember of my high school German wouldn't even get us safely through buying a meal."

Carlos joined gaily in her laughter, his handsome face infinitely attractive in this lighthearted mood.

"Then in Berlin I shall have to serve as your interpreter again."

"You speak German too?"

"Mais oui. French, German, Italian, English, a smattering of Russian, and of course Spanish, my native tongue. We Europeans are not as insular as you Americans, you know. We are not shielded on either side by an ocean, as you are. Rather, we live surrounded by neighboring countries. It becomes a matter of necessity that we attempt to understand and be understood."

I only wish I could understand and be understood by you, Anne thought suddenly, wistfully. A wave of dismay ran through her as she faced how impossible this was. Greater barriers than not sharing the same language separated her from Carlos. Even if she buckled down to learn every language he spoke, there would still remain an impassable gulf of differing culture and social class between them.

Carlos dropped her arm and his hand caught hers. "So for today we are friends, right? We push out of our minds all thought of enmity and simply become tourists ready to enjoy Paris, the city that many people consider the loveliest and most romantic in the world. Is that agreed?"

As Anne's eyes held his, she nodded her assent. Carlos gave her fingers a friendly squeeze and flashed her a warm smile.

"Good enough. And I guarantee one thing, my little American friend. If you will place yourself solely and trustfully in my hands, I shall promise you this: Today will be so crowded with beautiful sights and sounds that by the time it is finally over, at dawn tomorrow, you will admit that it was the most enjoyable and unforgettable day of your life."

As Carlos's glittering black eyes met hers, Anne wanted to laugh but found she couldn't. A fear had risen to block her laughter. The best she could do was smile shyly back at him. It wasn't that she feared Carlos couldn't deliver what he had promised. What she feared was that he could.

Chapter Five

The day passed in a kaleidoscope of sights and sounds, with an amazing amount of spontaneous, carefree laughter. Carlos, relaxed and friendly, was the most wonderful companion Anne had ever known or even imagined. Had she not clung fiercely, tenaciously, to her knowledge of what he was really like as a person, she would have fallen hopelessly in love with him.

Carlos drove them first to what he called the most famous boulevard in the world, the Avenue des Champs-Élysées. They sat at a small table in a sidewalk café, enjoying a continental breakfast, watching the endless traffic stream by on the multi-lane avenue that was for Anne the embodiment of every romantic postcard she'd ever seen of Paris. As they finished their breakfast, Carlos pulled her eagerly to her feet and asked her how energetic a walker she was.

"We must walk for a time," he insisted. "Only by walking can we get a real feel for this most historic and textured of cities. And a walk of two miles is nothing, *n'est-ce pas?*"

Two miles! Anne instinctively opened her mouth

to protest, but at sight of Carlos's eager, challenging grin, she found herself smiling in return and nodding. As Carlos took her arm and led her off, he murmured encouragingly, "We will walk briskly to save time and to make the distance disappear rapidly beneath our feet, *non?* Surely in your young days as a Girl Scout you often hiked far more than a mere two miles, isn't that so?"

"But I was never a Girl Scout!" Anne protested.

Carlos stopped walking and stared at her in surprise. "But I thought all good little American girls were Girl Scouts!"

Amused by his intent expression, Anne replied laughingly, "Well, maybe I was never a good little girl. Have you thought of that?"

Carlos's black eyes fixed on hers, and a warmly teasing glint came into them. "Ah, but of course you were! It is only since you've become grown and have seen too many gangster movies that you've let yourself be dragged down into sly and reprobate ways."

"Of course," Anne agreed, and as Carlos grasped her arm more firmly to lead her forward again, they laughed together.

"My knowledge of English is quite good, is it not?" Carlos asked a moment later. " 'Sly and reprobate ways,' " he quoted himself. "Even in your language I am adept at turning a facile phrase, is this not so?"

"Indeed, yes," Anne responded agreeably, touched that Carlos should care enough to seek a compliment from her. Maybe he was not quite as arrogantly sure of himself as he seemed. "One can easily tell that while you may be a marine engineer by profession, at heart you are a lover and poet."

Anne made this comment in a lighthearted, teasing tone, and certainly meant no offense. She was surprised that Carlos glanced immediately around with a suddenly sober expression, black eyes shadowed.

"Ah, but you're wrong," he muttered. "Above all else, at heart I am my father's son, and nothing matters more to me than family honor, family pride. Don't ever fool yourself that this is not so."

How could I possibly fool myself? Anne thought irritably, her own eyes darkening. For a moment there, laughing and joking together, she and Carlos had gotten too close. He was warning her to pull back, keep her distance, to remember at all times who he was and who she was. Their agreed-upon pact of friendliness for the day meant only the cessation of active hostilities, not that a groundwork could be laid for a truly warm friendship. *I'll keep that in mind and won't trespass again,* Anne told herself.

Carlos guided her first to the Place de la Concorde, at the southeastern end of the Champs-Élysées. This was the square, he informed her, where the guillotine stood during the Reign of Terror.

"Glance around now at all the people hurrying through, at the pleasant harmonious aspect here, and there is little to remind you that it was at one time the notorious Place de la Guillotine, splashing with the blood of over one thousand three hundred victims of the Revolution."

"There certainly isn't," Anne agreed, but nonetheless she shivered and felt momentarily cold.

She gazed up in awe at the Obelisk of Luxor, a two-hundred-ton stone needle from Egypt that had been erected in the square in 1836. Carlos led her over to where she could catch a breathtaking view of the Tuileries Garden, framed by the winged horses of Coysevox, down through the little Arc de Triomphe du Carrousel to the Louvre. Then he swung her around and again they faced the broad boulevard of the Champs-Élysées.

"Now we shall begin our two-mile walk along the most enchanting boulevard in Europe to the world-famous Arc de Triomphe, a monument that every tourist in Paris absolutely must visit. You can already see it there at the other end of the boulevard, at the Place Charles de Gaulle, formerly known as the Étoile, or Star. When we arrive there you will understand why it was known as the Étoile, as no fewer than twelve avenues radiate out from it like rays of light from a star. In the center of the Place is the Arc de Triomphe, which is a hundred and sixty-four feet high, more than twice the size of the Arch of Constantine in Rome. Under the Arc burns a perpetual light dedicated to France's Unknown Soldier. When we arrive there, we will take an elevator to the top for a most splendid view of this magnificent city."

As they walked along the boulevard, Carlos held on to her arm and Anne felt caught up in the romance and mystery of this most beloved of cities. During their walk Carlos said little, but when they reached their destination, he asked her how she was faring.

"Your feet are not yet hurting, I hope?"

"You are right, they are not."

"I'm glad," Carlos said. "Before I ever suggested this walk I had noticed, of course, that you are not one of those silly women who put fashion over comfort and wear those ridiculous shoes with heels tall and thin enough to go through concrete."

"Spike heels, you mean?" Anne suggested, laughing.

"Ah, is that what they're called?" Carlos laughed, his black eyes twinkling as he motioned toward the city below. "But is this not an enchanting view of a most enchanting city?"

And most enchanting company too, Anne felt an impulse to say, but she forced herself to refrain, answering simply, "Yes, indeed it is."

After they'd seen the view from the top of the Arc de Triomphe and had spent a few minutes wandering through the exhibition there, they descended to the ground and Carlos said that, to save some time, as well as to conserve their energy, they wouldn't walk back up the avenue to where he'd parked his car. Instead they would catch a cab. They must go to the Louvre next, of course, the largest palace in the world and surely also the world's greatest and most famous art gallery and museum.

Their stay at the Louvre was relatively brief for Carlos was anxious that they have time to go through

73

the Tuileries Garden and visit the Jeu de Paume, a museum housing a fantastic collection of impressionist paintings.

"Ah, the impressionists," Carlos remarked as they entered the Jeu de Paume. "I don't know about your tastes in art, of course, but I have a special love for the impressionists, and Van Gogh is my number-one favorite artist of all time. His colors, his vibrant, vibrant colors! Ah, yes. When I am here in Paris on business, and find myself forced to kill a few hours—that is how you Americans phrase it, yes?—when I am frustrated in what I am trying to accomplish, I come here and stand once again before these paintings and all irritation, all anger, seems to melt away."

Carlos sighed. His hand fell away from Anne's arm but he flashed her a friendly, dismayed little smile. "Businessmen all over the world know about red tape, of course, the complicated, often contradictory regulations that governments issue, the infuriating delay of having to deal with an endless army of bureaucrats, but no other nation can frustrate one as can this glorious Republic of France. Businessmen from all over the world, when forced to deal with the French, admit to that. In America one needs a knife to cut through the red tape, yes? In France a knife would be useless. Instead you must use an armored tank."

Carlos slanted her an amused glance. "It is, to put it very gently and kindly, a most depressingly frustrating experience. So when I find myself ready to steam up and boil over, I force myself to come here, to immerse myself in these magnificent works. And slowly I remind myself that a nation that could produce the impressionists—Manet, Monet, Seurat, Degas, and especially that fantastic genius, the post-impressionist Van Gogh—can't be all bad."

After a slight hesitation, Anne dared say, "But—Van Gogh was Dutch, not French, wasn't he?"

Carlos burst out with a happy laugh, momentarily clasping Anne's hand in his. His black eyes twinkled merrily. "Ah, I wondered if you would catch that, but of course you did. Yes, Van Gogh was Dutch. Nevertheless, he did much of his best work while living in the south of France, he was greatly influenced by the French impressionists, and his brother Theo, who supported him most of his life, lived and worked in Paris. Surely he can be considered at least an adopted son of France, *n'est-ce pas?*"

"Of course, if you wish," Anne murmured, and as Carlos grinned broadly at her she smiled back, feeling an odd tension suddenly grip her. Carlos, smiling or sober, laughing or scowling, friendly or hostile, was such an incredibly handsome, appealing man, it hurt at moments even to look at him, to have him so physically close yet not close enough. Anne was reminded of pictures she'd seen of poor children with their noses pressed against windows as they eyed fabulous goodies they could not have. In spite of her great efforts at control, there were moments with Carlos when she felt a painful kinship with those hungry children.

When they left the Jeu de Paume, they agreed it was past time for lunch. Carlos asked her with a smile whether she'd prefer an elegant or casual atmosphere. Before she'd had a chance to decide, he suggested with a boyish grin that they try casual for lunch and save elegant for dinner.

"Fine with me," Anne responded, grinning too, her pulse racing to hear that Carlos planned to stay with her at least through dinner. What a fabulous day he was giving her!

They had lunch at the Bar des Théâtres across from the Plaza-Athénée, an inexpensive place that Carlos told her excitedly was a favorite of models, actresses and their legions of male admirers. While they were lunching, Carlos cast a number of interested glances at the tall, voluptuous, heavily made-up young women.

Royalty often formed informal alliances with actresses and showgirl types, Anne thought rather sadly to herself; but, then, so did many men who didn't have a drop of royal blood. She could feel herself becoming withdrawn, irrationally resenting Carlos's obvious admiration for the glittery, glamorous young Frenchwomen laughing and chattering gaily on every side. Why should she care what kind of woman Carlos found most attractive? She had known from the first that he was not a man she could ever win for herself. Nor did she want to win him, she hastily reminded herself.

After lunch, they visited the Eiffel Tower, drove past the Luxembourg Gardens, passed the Sorbonne and wound up at the Notre-Dame cathedral. Wandering through the cathedral, Anne felt all but overwhelmed. Unexpected tears came to her eyes as she stared at the glorious stained-glass windows, especially the rose window, which Carlos whispered to her was seven hundred years old. Carlos asked her, also in a whisper, whether she felt up to climbing to the top of the tower. "It's a pretty stiff climb," he warned her, eyeing her with concern. "If you'd rather not, just say so, and we won't."

"Oh, no. I'm not feeling overly tired and I'd like to, really."

It was already twilight when they reached the tower, and the lights of Paris were beginning to sparkle below. Anne sighed at the magnificent view spread out all around them. Carlos, standing beside her, momentarily put his arm around her waist. "It's almost too beautiful a sight to bear, isn't it?" he suggested, in a softly subdued voice.

As she glanced around to agree, Anne thought, *But, no. I can bear the sight of beautiful, romantic Paris, as lovely as it is; it's having you so near and knowing you will always be out of reach that is unbearable.* Her eyes stung with a hot mist as she nervously moved away, and Carlos dropped his arm, as though rebuffed.

After they climbed down from the tower and left the cathedral, they strolled for an hour along the banks of the Seine. "No tourist who comes to Paris, even if only for a day, should miss this," Carlos said. They passed numerous young people sitting on the banks of the river; some were earnestly conversing, while others were embracing and kissing. Here and there were artists planted before their easels, attempting to catch the last faint glimmers of twilight before giving up and going home. The river, flowing smoothly along, glittered with reflected light and Anne wondered whether this wasn't the most beautiful sight she had seen all day.

"Shall we take a cruise along the river?" Carlos suggested with sudden inspiration. "I've taken it during the day but never at night. What do you say?"

"Sounds wonderful. I'd love to."

The cruise was marvelous. It was fully dark by the time they climbed board the launch at the Pont d'Iéna for the three-mile journey to the Île de la Cité. Paris sparkled before them. As Anne stood leaning over the upper rail, Carlos beside her, she allowed herself to drift into a fantasy that the incredibly handsome, charming man at her side was her husband, and this was their honeymoon. Had she not known Carlos for what he really was—an arrogantly self-righteous and unscrupulous man hiding behind a well-mannered façade—she could so easily have fallen in love with him. Even more, she would have found it impossible *not* to fall in love with him.

By the time they disembarked from the launch, in the shadows of the great Notre-Dame de Paris, it was twenty-five after nine.

"A fashionably late hour for dinner, and to tell the truth I'm starved," Carlos said with a smile, and Anne immediately agreed that she was hungry too.

"For lunch we sampled the casual. Tonight we shall indulge in the elegant," Carlos announced, black eyes twinkling.

Anne feared that the light blue blouse and simple tailored suit she wore wouldn't do for an elegant restaurant and suggested they return to her *pension* first.

"Nonsense," Carlos replied. "You look just fine. Certainly you are every bit as elegantly dressed as I am. The restaurant I have in mind is one I often go to and everyone knows me. They'll greet us with open arms and give us excellent service, believe me."

The Chez Denis, on the Avenue Gustave Flaubert, surprised Anne with its unpretentious exterior and completely unspectacular interior. When Carlos caught the look of surprise on her face, he leaned over to whisper into her ear, "Don't be fooled by the appearance, Anne. The cuisine is delicious, the service first rate, and the prices astronomically high, but worth it. You'll see."

At a few minutes after eleven Anne sipped the last of her after-dinner cordial and happily admitted to Carlos that she was full to bursting with the best dinner she had ever had.

"Anne, I hate to rush you," Carlos murmured politely in response, smiling, "but there is something else I wish to show you and I'm afraid it's getting late. If we rush we will just make it."

After a terrifyingly quick ride in a cab, the quickest way to where they were going, Carlos said, they drew up in front of a magnificent building which Carlos informed Anne was the Opera, the largest theatrical building in the world. When Carlos sought admittance, he was told that it was far too late, the evening's performance was all but over.

"Ah, but we just wish to go within to see the building itself," Carlos explained, and after a few banknotes had changed hands, he and Anne were admitted.

As they stood in the main foyer, Anne felt overwhelmed by the grand staircase they faced.

"Magnificent, is it not?" Carlos whispered into her ear, and Anne nodded in awed agreement.

Before long, they caught a cab back to where Carlos had earlier parked his little rented car, and Anne felt sure that their delightful day of sightseeing was now over. Carlos would surely return her to her undistinguished little room in the *pension*, where tomorrow she would receive Michael's call. But Carlos, flashing her a conspiratorial smile, assured her that he had other plans.

"The night is still young, *ma chère*." Reaching for Anne's hand, he gave it a squeeze. Anne felt her heart instantly race at both the endearment and the way Carlos's hand momentarily clasped hers. If only he weren't who he was, the rich, noble, dreadful man she knew him to be!

At one o'clock in the morning, they began a fast whirl through the Left Bank nightclubs. "We met in a nightclub in Morocco," Carlos reminded Anne with a grin. "Now we will see what this most enchanting of cities has to offer for entertainment. After all, no tourist can claim he has seen the real Paris until he has been to *les boîtes*. Are you game?"

Anne hesitated momentarily, but felt herself being carried away by Carlos's wide challenging grin and the excited gleam of his deep black eyes. "Well, yes, I guess so, if you like."

"Good enough."

They crowded into dark little nightclubs where cigar and cigarette smoke hung so thickly in the air it was hard to breathe, pushed their way onto tiny floors so packed with people it was all but impossible to dance; the best they could do was move their feet and sway their bodies in rhythm to the loud, insistent beat. They danced until they were so exhausted they had to sit, and then they watched the exotically dressed people who swarmed around them.

It was dawn as they left one club and began walking wearily arm in arm down the street. The sun was not yet visible in the sky, but the air was clear and crisp.

"Carlos, surely we have now had enough," Anne suggested, glancing around at him and feeling very bleary eyed.

Carlos's eyes met hers, and he burst out laughing. Putting an arm around her waist, he gave her a little squeeze. *"Oui, ma chère,* even I have had enough. Time to go home."

As Carlos drove them slowly through the nearly deserted streets, Anne rested her head back and almost fell asleep. What a fantastic twenty or so hours this had been! Anne knew that she had accumulated memories that would grow even richer over the years, but for the moment all she wanted was to crawl into bed and fall asleep.

When they reached the *pension* where she was staying, Carlos parked his car and walked her into the little entry hall. There he reached for one hand and held it as he gazed down at her.

"Well, dear Anne, it was worth it, was it not? Putting aside our hostility for one day to enjoy the city? I promised you a day you would never forget. Have I made good on my promise?"

In spite of her exhaustion, Anne felt a wave of affection and excitement wash through her. How charming Carlos could be when he chose!

She leaned forward to press a soft kiss on Carlos's cheek. "Yes, you more than made good on your promise. You gave me a day such as I have never experienced before and quite likely never will again, for which I thank you."

"And I thank you," Carlos responded softly. He reached out, put his arms around her and drew her close. Anne felt so tired she instinctively rested her head on Carlos's shoulder as he held her. How warm and comforting his nearness was! They stood unmoving for several seconds, then as Anne lifted her head to pull away, Carlos drew her even closer. His sensuous mouth pressed down on hers. Anne felt her pulse speed up. She lifted her arms and slipped them around Carlos's neck. Their kiss slowly deepened, Carlos moving his lips against hers to urge them open. As he tasted the soft sweetness within she gave a little moan, tangling her fingers in the luxuriant dark hair at his nape. His answering groan caused Anne to shiver and tremble with excitement. Of her own accord she pressed even harder against him, to where she could feel his hard masculine strength moving, breathing against her. As their kiss ended at last, as Carlos slowly, erotically withdrew from her, Anne thought this seemed the perfect way to end their day.

Finally each drew back, as though in accord, and stood a moment gazing steadily at the other.

"Thank you again, Anne. I had a truly wonderful time." Carlos spoke softly in his full, deep voice.

Anne felt happy and tired and bewildered and excited all at the same time. "I'm the one who thanks you," she murmured in response.

A door opened onto the entryway and the tiny white-haired woman who ran the *pension* peered out, bright old eyes appraising them. Anne drew back, murmured one final, "Thank you," and turned to begin ascending the stairs. She heard Carlos address her landlady, but as he spoke in French she would not have understood his words even had she lingered to listen, which she didn't. All she wanted now was to make it up the stairs to her second-floor room.

She had just finished undressing and turning down her bed when there was a rap on the door and Carlos's voice called out, "Anne? Anne, you aren't asleep yet, are you?"

Startled, momentarily frightened, Anne walked over to the door without opening it. "Carlos, what do you want? Why are you here?" Her pulse raced with both excitement and unreasonable fear.

"Open the door, please, Anne. I want to tell you something, that's all. I know how tired you are but it's quite important, really. If it weren't, I wouldn't be bothering you."

Anne unlocked the door and opened it. As she did so, she became acutely aware that she wore only a flimsy nightgown. Why hadn't she grabbed up a coat or robe to cover herself? Carlos's black eyes met her startled gaze, fastened on her figure, moving quickly, appraisingly, up and down her too exposed form.

"All right, Carlos, what is it?" Anne demanded rather tartly, embarrassed for herself and angry at Carlos for making it even worse. If he didn't stop looking at her that way, she would close the door in his face!

Carlos's eyes came up to meet hers again, sparkling with amusement. "Forgive me, *ma chère,* but I just wanted to tell you that I made arrangements with the landlady to rent the room down the hall here, which fortunately happens to be vacant. I also explained to her that you are expecting an extremely important long-distance call sometime today and asked her to wake you for the call even if it comes within the next few hours. I asked that she also wake me when the call comes, as I wish to be present when you speak to your brother."

By this time Carlos's face had hardened into a sober, almost stern expression, and the flirtatious sparkle had died completely out of his eyes. "And now I bid you good night, dear Anne," he ended in a coolly businesslike voice. He offered her a formal little bow before he walked away down the narrow hall.

As Anne watched him leave, she felt a sudden, sinking despair. Carlos had suggested a one-day truce in their personal war and that's all it had been, a temporary halt in hostilities, but now the war was on again. His face had showed it, as had his voice. Once again she was his enemy, as he was hers. Sighing, blinking back weary, discouraged tears, Anne closed the door and padded barefooted across her small room to the bed. She hoped she would get a few hours' sleep at least before Michael phoned and the cold war burst into a hot war again. It was a war she felt certain in her heart that she and her brother were bound to lose. How could it be otherwise, when commoners dared to challenge royalty?

Chapter Six

Michael's call came a little after eleven that morning. Anne, wearing nightgown, robe, and slippers, stood in the narrow, drafty downstairs hall with the phone receiver plastered painfully against her ear. Their connection was bad and each tried to compensate by shouting. Carlos stood only a few feet away, leaning elegantly against the wall, his handsome face coldly impassive.

Michael began by announcing jubilantly that Anne could now fly home. "We're all set, sis," Michael shouted. "Dorrie's got her passport and we're booked for a flight this evening. We don't know how to thank you for helping us, but it's all over now and you're free to fly home. Dorrie says to— No, wait, she wants to speak to you herself."

"Anne." Dorrie's soft voice could barely be heard through all the static. "Thank you, dear Anne."

"I can hardly hear you," Anne shouted back, her head buzzing, whirling with fatigue. "Can *you* hear *me?* There's something important I've got to tell Michael."

Her brother came back on the line and Anne felt

hot tears splash into her eyes as she told him of Carlos's plan. "If you don't return his sister to their home, he's going to the police, Michael. He's going to swear out a warrant for your arrest, on the charge of grand theft. He'll claim you stole, or helped Dorrie to steal, that jewelry she took and—"

"But I didn't!" Michael shouted. "That's a lie! I didn't even know Dorrie had taken the stuff until we'd crossed into Morocco. Besides that, no one stole that jewelry; it belongs to her. How dare Carlos accuse me of stealing it?"

Anne glanced down the hall to where Carlos stood, her tired, hurting eyes focusing on his haughty, impassive face, and she felt even more ready to crumple down into hopeless sobs. But she refused to give him the satisfaction of seeing her cry!

"Michael, I know all that," she shouted into the mouthpiece, "but Carlos says the police won't bother him over trivialities, that they'll issue the warrant now and worry about the details later. He says he's tired of chasing you himself and is ready to sit back and let the police find you for him. So—what do you want me to do? What shall I tell him?"

"The son of a—" Michael's angry voice faded away, then a moment later he spoke up more clearly again. "Well, tell him he wins. We'll cancel our flight home and return to Spain instead, unless you want us to fly to Paris and meet you there. If Carlos is agreeable to that, that's what we'll do. If he's right there, can you ask him? Will he hold off on going to the police if we agree to fly to Paris on the first flight we can get?"

"Hold on and I'll ask him." As Anne started to

lower the receiver, however, she heard Dorrie's voice again, sounding frantic and tearful, so she lifted the receiver to press it against her ear once more.

"No, Anne," Dorrie begged, "don't tell my brother any such thing. We're flying to America, not back to Spain or Paris or anywhere else. Tell my brother that! Tell him he can make any threats he likes but he can't win. I won't let him win. I love Michael and he loves me and we're flying out tonight to the United States. Tell him that, Anne. Tell him there's no way in this world he can drag me back home!"

"But, Dorrie," Anne protested, blinking furiously against the tired tears swarming into her eyes.

For the next five minutes the three of them argued fruitlessly back and forth. Michael, obviously sobered by the thought of going to jail, was in favor of meeting Carlos in Paris at once, especially after he heard that Carlos intended to keep Anne with him until the jewelry and his sister were safely restored. Dorrie, however, was nearly hysterical at the thought of returning to her family and refused to be persuaded. Helplessly, Anne listened to first one and then the other, despairing of their ever coming to an agreement. Finally she could stand no more.

"I think you'd better talk directly to Carlos," Anne suggested to her brother, and glancing down at Carlos again she extended the phone receiver. With a slow, arrogant smile, Carlos walked up and took the receiver she held out.

"Yes, this is Carlos," he said very coldly and formally into the phone.

Her head now throbbing with pain, Anne leaned

back against the wall, closed her eyes and pressed her hands against her brow. Carlos did not say anything for several moments. When next he spoke, it was in Spanish, so Anne concluded that Dorrie was again on the line. For several minutes Carlos carried on an animated conversation with his sister, then with a small, cold smile he hung up the phone and faced Anne.

"They are not of one mind, as you no doubt know, these impetuous lovers who so romantically adore each other, and then begin fighting and screaming at each other with the very first crisis they face. And this will lead to an enduring, happy marriage, of course!" Carlos's sneering smile broadened. "My sister claims to believe I am only uttering empty threats, but even she knows better than that. However, if you wish to accept her word for it and fly home today, that is your choice, of course."

Anne stared wearily into Carlos's arrogantly gleaming black eyes. "And—if I do—?"

"I shall go to the police, as I told you, without delay. Your brother seems upset by this prospect, but who is to say whether he will win out over my childish, willful, bad-tempered sister? However, I am a reasonably patient man and told her over the phone just now that I would give them one week to iron out their clash of wills and come to some resolution. If they ignore my warning and fly to the United States to get married, I shall of course go to the police and swear out a warrant at once. Or if they return to our home in Palencia, I will bid you a fond farewell and see that you are not further delayed in returning home yourself." Carlos paused, flashing out a coldly triumphant smile. "Does that clarify the situation for you, *ma chère?*"

"Yes," Anne murmured with a sigh of resignation. "How soon are we leaving Paris?"

Carlos's smile broadened into a friendlier one of affectionate concern. "Oh, not today, surely. We are both too tired. I suggest that you take it easy for the meantime, rest as much as you can, and then we will leave early tomorrow morning. I shall return to my hotel, shower, change, rest myself, and prepare for our departure. So I won't see you until around eight tomorrow morning unless—unless you'd care to have dinner with me tonight?" he ended on a softer, warmer note.

Anne's tired eyes flashed back at him. She felt an impulse to snap out that no, thank you, dinner with him was the very last thing she wanted, but as she opened her mouth to reply she couldn't ignore the sudden, excited racing of her pulse. "All right," she murmured, dismayed at herself, "that would be nice. I'd appreciate it."

"My pleasure," Carlos replied with a courtly little bow. "Seven o'clock, shall we say? I shall see you then." He swung around and walked away down the narrow hall.

He was extremely punctual that evening, rapping softly on her door at seven o'clock sharp. Anne, wearing a soft blue off-the-shoulder dress, greeted him with a nervous smile, pleased and flattered to see his black eyes light up.

"Ah, but how lovely you look!" As though half in mockery of himself, Carlos leaned over her hand to kiss it. As his head lifted again, he flashed her a boyish grin. "Just because we are mortal enemies, there is nothing to prevent us from liking and enjoying each other, *n'est-ce pas?*"

As Carlos broke into a soft laugh, Anne laughed too. "All right, if you say so," she agreed, her cheeks flushing a becoming pink.

They ate dinner at a noisy, crowded restaurant on the Boulevard du Montparnasse, which Carlos informed her had been a favorite haunt of her fellow American, Ernest Hemingway. After dinner they went for a leisurely drive, then Carlos parked so that they could again take a stroll along the banks of the Seine. The evening before it had been twilight as they walked along the riverbank; tonight it was fully dark. Couples were everywhere, walking, sitting, lying on the riverbank in feverish embrace. Carlos suggested after they'd walked for a time that they sit themselves. Anne rather self-consciously agreed. In spite of herself she felt a little shiver run down her spine, more from tension than the cold, but Carlos, noticing, was immediately solicitous. He slipped out of his jacket and draped it over her shoulders, then, holding onto the lapels, drew her forward and kissed her.

"How charming you have looked all evening, with your pale, golden-brown hair and those blue, blue eyes," he murmured. "No wonder my sister has lost her head over your brother if he is as handsome as you are lovely." His hands holding her shoulders, he pulled her to him and kissed her again, a longer, more ardent kiss. After the kiss, he moved her so that she sat in front of him, resting back against his lean, hard frame while his arms loosely encircled her.

For some time they sat like this, neither speaking, then Carlos suddenly remarked in a low, bemused tone, "You know, *ma chère*, this may be impossible for you to believe, but sometimes I wish I too were an American." He interrupted himself with a soft laugh. "But maybe it is only that each of us at times entertains himself with the fantasy of being someone other than who he is. Possibly at times you have dreamed of being European, is that not so?"

Glancing around, Anne laughed too. "Well, possibly," she agreed, though at the moment she couldn't recall that she ever had.

"Not only European but royal, I'd wager." There was a hint of amusement in his voice, as if he was laughing at the thought of a mere commoner having such lofty daydreams. Before Anne could deny it, he pulled her around and kissed her, with greater passion than ever before.

As dismay washed through her, Anne fought against responding to the kiss, fought against the racing of her pulse, the quick, excited stirring of her blood. Even in his friendliest mood, the warmly intimate mood he was now in, Carlos nevertheless always managed to remind her of the difference in their stations in life, to warn her anew of the impassable gulf between them. He might willingly share a few kisses with an attractive young American he found physically pleasing, but never would he consider sharing his name with her, or his life. *Stay away from him!* Anne sternly ordered, and she pulled herself out of Carlos's arms the moment she could.

After he drove her home around midnight, Carlos bade her a friendly farewell in the downstairs entryway, reminding her that he would pick her up around eight the next morning for their journey south.

"Meanwhile, sweet dreams," he murmured, touching his warm lips softly to her cheek as he bade her good night.

Anne found herself repeatedly sighing as she climbed the stairs to her room. The thought of the next day, the next few days, was frightening to contemplate. But somehow she'd keep her cool, hold Carlos at arm's length, and escape unscathed, with both her heart and her virtue intact. It wouldn't be easy, she knew, but nevertheless it could be done. And she would do it.

Carlos arrived right on time the following morning, punctual as always. As he carried her one bag out and put it into the trunk of his small rented car, Anne studied his face, surprised to note his impassive expression, the renewed coldness in his eyes. As she climbed into the car, she swung to face him.

"Did you rest well last night?" she asked, wishing she could think of a less inane remark to begin the conversation.

Carlos's black eyes shot around to confront her. He opened his mouth as though to say something, then shut it firmly. After he'd started the motor and swung the small car out into the road, he finally answered without glancing her way.

"I slept well enough, thank you. But I feel I should tell you something. Last night after I bade you good night, I returned to my hotel to find a message from my father requesting that I phone home. When I brought my father and my aunt up to date on this impossible situation, they were both upset. They feel I should go directly to the police rather than give your brother time to possibly change his name and go underground, dragging my sister with him. They consider it highly foolish of me to wait even a day. Although I discussed it with them for half an hour, trying to get them to see the wisdom of the course I am pursuing, I could not persuade them. They continued to argue with me and, in fact, threatened to go to the police themselves if I did not do so at once."

"And—?" Anne prodded, when Carlos fell silent again. He drove staring straight ahead at the road, his handsome face set in a scowl.

"What have you decided to do?" Anne prodded again a moment later, when Carlos still hadn't answered.

At last Carlos glanced around, gleaming black eyes shooting angry sparks at her. "I will proceed with the plan we have agreed upon," he snapped irritably. "You will find that I am every bit as stubborn as my sister and no more willing than she to bow down under threats. Regardless of what my father and aunt claim, I do not for a minute believe they will go to the police. I told your brother I would give him a week. I shall give him a week. After that—well, we shall see."

Once again Carlos fell silent. Anne, after watching him for a minute or two, drew her eyes away and began absently watching the road. Their truce was now a thing of the past, obviously. The battle was on again, she an unwilling, unhappy prisoner of war. Or—was she?

"I made another phone call this morning," Carlos said suddenly, his cool voice exploding in the tense silence, "that possibly will make you angry, possibly not. I hope it won't. As I mentioned to you once, I manage the family marine engineering firm. Ever since I ended my schooling, I have put all my time and energy into the business. Often I have gone for weeks without taking even a weekend off, much less a day during the week.

"I'm not complaining," he threw in, flashing Anne a quick smile. "I enjoy my work tremendously and take pride in the fact that I have doubled the profits of the company in the ten years since I took it over. But enough is enough. When my sister ran away, naturally I had to break off all business activity until I could find her. But now that I firmly believe she will return why should I rush back to work? So I have decided to take a few days off, during which time we will enjoy ourselves before returning to my home. I made a phone call this morning, as I just mentioned, to a young American couple I know who spend this time of year at their villa on the French Riviera. They've invited us there for some leisurely swimming, sunning, and relaxation. I hope you won't mind that I accepted their invitation without consulting you."

"Mind?" Anne's head spun with this new development. "But—but what if Michael and your sister

94

resolve their argument and head straight home? There we'll be, sunning ourselves on the Riviera, while they cool their heals in Palencia waiting for us. That doesn't make sense!"

"No?" Carlos snapped, irritated eyes swinging around to glare at her. "In the first place, I know my sister and she won't give in that easily."

"And I know my brother," Anne countered hotly, "and he will do what he thinks is right regardless of your sister!"

"Even if we delay a week, we will still beat them home!" Carlos insisted.

"Well, even if you're right, I can't just stay over here week after week. Maybe you have a vacation coming but mine will soon be over. What excuse can I give my boss for not returning, that I'm lolling around on the beach with a Spanish duke? He'd never believe that!"

"Then tell him I've kidnapped you!" Carlos suggested, his handsome face breaking into a broad grin. He glanced around, black eyes gleaming with amusement. "Tell him I'm a terrorist, that I'm holding you hostage while my confederates collect a million dollars in ransom for you. Or—"

"Oh, he'd believe that, of course!" Anne interrupted, but she couldn't keep from laughing herself. "But, seriously, Carlos," she pleaded as their laughter died away, "I'm just not equipped for even a day on the beach. I came over here on a rescue mission for my brother, remember, and I packed only this linen dress, my suit, and the blue dress I wore last night. No bathing suit, no leisure clothes, nothing for a stay on the beach. I don't like the beach anyway," she added moodily. "I don't tan properly, I just burn, then the burn fades away into stupid red freckles. Ever since I was twelve years old I've hated beaches and I never go to one, with anyone."

"Ah, but you must with me," Carlos murmured affectionately, and his hand came over to catch up hers. "Number one, we can buy you a swimsuit and leisure clothes. Number two, what if you do freckle? I'm sure you'd look delightful with freckles. Number three, no tourist can leave France without first visiting the famous Riviera. Number four, I've already phoned these American friends, as I told you, and they're expecting us. If you don't like swimming, we'll go sailing instead. Or waterskiing. Or just lie around on the beach. Or we'll sleep all day and go to the casino every night. Or go dancing at the nightclubs."

Carlos drew the car to a stop at a light and swung around to face Anne. "To be truthful, Anne, I haven't been to the Riviera myself in almost fifteen years. The last time I went I was still a boy. When this chance seemed to present itself, I couldn't resist. Please say you'll come along with me. I promised you a good time in Paris and I delivered, did I not? Now I promise you an equally good time at St. Tropez. Two or three days enjoying ourselves, and when we both agree we've had enough, we'll speed on home. And I'll wager anything you'd like to bet that we still arrive there before Dolores and your brother."

Smiling, her pulse racing, Anne countered softly, "But—Carlos, what if you never agree that you've had enough? Let's at least put a definite time limit on our stay."

"Fair enough!" Carlos grinned companionably. "Suggest a limit and we'll negotiate."

"Two hours," Anne murmured teasingly.

"Two weeks!" came the swift reply.

"Two days."

"One week."

"Three days."

"All right, three days. Shake on it?" Though he kept his eyes carefully on the road, Carlos put out his hand to her.

As Anne slipped her hand into his and shook it, she told herself that she hadn't lost anything. Three days out of her life, and even if Carlos was wrong and Michael and Dorrie were already in Palencia by the time she and Carlos arrived, it really wouldn't matter that much. She'd make sure that Carlos phoned home each day so that Michael, should he arrive before them, would at least know where she was, and that she was perfectly all right. But, Anne wondered suddenly, frowning, would she *be* perfectly all right? How many days, and nights, could she spend with this handsome, charming, arrogant, baffling man, and still keep her heart intact?

Chapter Seven

Three exciting, fun-filled, sun-drenched days on the Riviera. When Anne looked back on them afterward, they seemed to her golden days, rich with laughter, warm with love. Yet nothing of any great significance happened during their stay—except that sometime during those three days she fell hopelessly, irretrievably in love with Carlos.

After leaving Paris, they drove at a fast, steady pace, with only an occasional stop to stretch their legs or take in nourishment, and they arrived in St. Tropez late that evening. Carlos had phoned ahead to let his friends know when they would arrive.

"I call them my American friends," Carlos explained with a smile, "though actually Renée is French. But after she married Bob, almost overnight she seemed to adopt her husband's casual manner, the friendly informality that most Americans seem to share. She sounded overjoyed when she heard we were coming. There were no hints that we should have given her greater warning, none of that refined chill which a Frenchwoman would have used to let me know I had overstepped the limits of good manners. How refreshing you Americans are in so many ways!"

"Why, thank you, kind sir." Anne smiled in response to Carlos's compliment.

Carlos's friends, Bob and Renée Rubio, were a handsome, outspoken couple who welcomed Anne with open arms. They both gave her a big hug, then Renée asked if Carlos and Anne wished to share a room.

"If you do, fine. If not, that's fine too. We should have asked when Carlos phoned, but we were both so delighted to hear you were coming, we forgot. So which shall it be, togetherness or otherwise?"

Cheeks flushing, Anne murmured that they'd prefer separate bedrooms. "We've only just met," she explained, feeling pressed to come up with some explanation.

Carlos grinned at this, obviously amused by her embarrassment. "I guess she doesn't feel we've known each other as long as I do," he laughed.

"Don't tease the poor girl," Renée admonished him affectionately. "I don't blame her for wanting to keep you at arm's length." She turned to a male servant and gave him directions in French as to where to deposit each suitcase. "We'll put you in separate but adjoining bedrooms in case you get better acquainted fast," she teased, winking at Carlos, "as a great many people here seem to do. Meet on the beach in the morning, swim together in the afternoon, and by night—well, you know what I mean. Oh, it's so good to see you, Carlos," she exclaimed, and gave him another spontaneous, enthusiastic hug.

After a light, tasty midnight supper, they were shown to their rooms, where they went promptly to bed.

When Anne admitted after breakfast the following morning that she hadn't brought a swimsuit, Renée looked momentarily startled. She quickly recovered, however, and assured Anne that that was no problem.

"We're about the same size. Close enough, anyway. And I have an abundance of swimsuits as well as shorts, slacks, tee shirts, beach towels, beach robes, sandals, anything you could possibly need. Come with me now and I'll give you dozens of things to choose from, then ten minutes to change and we'll all troop down to the beach. Last one ready to go has to kick off his sandals and go barefooted."

"Sadist!" her husband muttered, and affectionately touseled her short reddish hair.

Swimming. Sunning. Sailing. Eating. Dancing. Gambling. Anne did her best to protect her fair skin from the sun, but she burned across her cheekbones, shoulders and upper arms in spite of all her precautions. The burn faded away into a delicate sprinkling of freckles. "See, I told you," she said to Carlos, annoyed with herself.

"And I told you you'd look just as beautiful," Carlos responded, "and you do." He bent to kiss one charmingly freckled shoulder, while Anne, laughing, did her best to pull away.

Later, driving in Bob's open car, wind blowing through her hair, face warm with leftover sun, the stars incredibly bright and close up above, Anne pushed out of her mind all thought of home, of work, of bills, of being poor. Above all she pushed away any thought of Michael or Dorrie. She tried to forget the bargain she and Carlos had made that they'd stay here only three days. Maybe if *she* forgot, Carlos would too.

The Rubios' villa, which was set on a promontory overlooking the beach, was a sprawling, white-washed structure surrounded by a low brick wall. The interior was an intriguing maze of low-ceilinged open rooms, casually yet tastefully furnished. Bob Rubio was a large, bluff man, his wife a slender, angular woman with pleasantly sharp features and bobbed red hair. They both did everything they could to make Anne feel welcome. In Paris Anne had found Carlos immensely attractive, but here on the Riviera he was even more devastating—not only friendly and charming, but relaxed and playful as well, ready to exert himself in every possible way to make sure that everyone enjoyed himself. Anne could feel her body relaxing, her spirits soaring, her heart expanding—it had to expand to make room for the joy-filled, hungry, frightening love she soon felt for Carlos.

On their third and final evening in St. Tropez, Carlos suggested to Anne that they go for a midnight swim. Though Renée and Bob were invited along, they both begged off. As the pair wound their way down the inclined path toward the beach, Carlos held Anne's hand, ostensibly to help guide and steady her. After they reached the sand, they dropped their towels and robes, then kicked off their sandals. With a grin, Carlos grabbed Anne's hand and pulled her toward the water while she tensed

101

against the shock of plunging into coldness. But, to her surprise, the water wasn't cold at all. Rather it was delightfully warm.

It was a lovely calm night, with an all but full moon hanging low in the sky. In the little cove they had chosen there were no breakers to worry about. Side by side they swam out some distance from the shore, then swung around and began swimming in. Before they'd reached shore again, Carlos swam in close beside Anne and grabbed hold of one leg. When Anne sputtered in surprise and began to sink, Carlos let go of her leg and grabbed her by the waist. Anne tried to pull free and they began to wrestle, coming up for air, splashing each other, laughing, playing. Anne's heart almost burst with the happiness she felt. After a time they swam in and walked up to where they'd left their gear. As Anne energetically rubbed herself dry, Carlos suggested they sit on the beach for a while before returning to the villa.

"It's so incredibly lovely out," Carlos murmured, glancing around. "It would be a shame to go inside right away."

They pulled on their beach robes, spread their towels on the sand, and sat a few feet apart, facing the sea. For quite some time they sat in companionable silence, while Anne realized that she'd never in her life felt as happy. No worry touched her, no thought of the morrow. There was only the moment, this surpassingly lovely night, with Carlos only a few feet away. Who could even have imagined a moment as perfect as this one?

"And thus ends our three days," Carlos murmured at last, smiling around at her, his deep full voice filled with regret.

Anne sighed, smiling softly back. "Ah, yes. But what a marvelous three days it's been."

"Agreed. Only I wish now I'd fought harder for a longer stay, a week perhaps."

"So do I," Anne admitted. As Carlos burst out with a soft laugh, she joined in.

As their laughter died away, Carlos moved over to sit beside her. "If we're both agreed on that—" But he left his thought unfinished as he drew her close and kissed her. How wonderfully soft and incredibly sweet his lips felt! Anne slid her arms around his shoulders and Carlos kissed her again, a touch more hungrily. As the kiss ended, Anne bowed her head, rested it against Carlos's shoulder, and let him draw her close. As her pulse began to race lightly, Anne murmured, "Maybe we should renegotiate—" Her soft voice was cut off by Carlos's finger pressed lightly against her lips.

"We'll see," Carlos answered, and kissed her again.

Time seemed to stop. Carlos's lips pressed harder, his tongue flicked against her mouth. Anne parted her lips slightly, her senses overwhelmed by the sheer maleness of him. As her heart beat ever harder, ever faster, he deepened the kiss, overriding any remaining resistance with the practiced ease of an experienced lover. Carlos's arms around her tightened and with a low moan of pleasure he swung her around to lie beneath him on the sand. His hands slid in under her beach robe, found the tie of her bikini bra, and with a quick pull unloosed it.

Oh, no, I must stop him! Anne thought feverishly, but she couldn't seem to gather her wits enough to act, to speak. Again Carlos kissed her, his mouth passionately demanding, his tongue thrusting hard and sure into her mouth. He tossed her bikini bra aside and his strong, warm hand came down on her breast, first lightly caressing the flesh, then cupping and pressing it.

At last the kiss ended, his grip on her loosening slightly as he drew away to gaze deeply into her eyes. Again Anne told herself frantically that she must stop him. She must order him to stop, right now. But again she couldn't seem to speak, or to act. Her heart beat terrifyingly fast, threatening to burst. Carlos, stretched out beside her, took her face in his hands and smiled down at her. His eyes seemed almost to be searching for something, so intent was his regard.

"Oh, Anne, *ma chère,* you're so lovely, so lovely," Carlos murmured, his voice low and hoarse. His fingertips moved slowly down her neck to lightly, teasingly trace the feminine outlines of her gently curving body. She shuddered as his lips followed the same path his hands had marked, leaving a trail of fire to her breasts. Anne heard his soft little moan of pleasure. One of her hands lifted, trembling, to press against his thick, silky black hair.

"Oh, Anne, Anne," Carlos cried softly.

The next moment Anne tensed against a sudden, almost painful wave of pleasure that threatened to engulf her as Carlos's mouth descended on the sensitive tip of one breast. How hot his tongue felt, how consuming—and suddenly she ached to be consumed by him.

Time had stopped. There was no time. There was only the nearly full moon climbing ever higher into the sky, the soft lapping of the water against the beach, the sweet-tangy scent of Carlos's luxuriant black hair still damp from their swim, his head bent over her, his mouth driving her on toward an ecstasy she had heretofore only dreamed of. *Oh Carlos I love you, oh, Carlos, what is happening to me!* Anne thought in frantic confusion, closing her eyes against the too beautiful sight of the big bright moon.

At last Carlos drew away, making a visible effort to bring his ragged breathing under control. Holding her against him in an embrace now free of passion, he waited while she gradually became aware once more of her whereabouts.

"Your skin is so very lovely and smooth," Carlos murmured. One hand began softly stroking her, her arm, her waist, the line of her hip, her thigh. Suddenly he said in a more businesslike tone, "But the breeze is getting a bit chilly and Renée and Bob will wonder what has happened to us. I suppose we ought to be getting back." He knelt beside her.

"Yes, I imagine we should." Reopening her eyes, Anne sat up, too. His black eyes met hers and for several seconds they gazed steadily at each other, Anne's pulse beating hard.

"You are so very, very lovely, Anne," Carlos said at last, in his deep, soft voice. "Whatever happens, I am glad we had these three days together."

"Yes," Anne whispered, her head whirling with

joy, with pain, with gratitude, with regret. *Carlos, I am so very glad too,* she wanted to say but couldn't. Her throat felt too tight, her voice seemed lost. *She* was lost too. Somehow during these soft, sweet, timeless days with Carlos she had lost herself. She had no idea now where she was, where she could find herself again. It filled her with dread, a deep, joyful dread.

Carlos stood up, handed her bikini top back, and Anne managed to get it clumsily retied. Carlos helped her up, they gathered their gear, and started up the path toward the villa. Once they reached level ground, Carlos walked closely beside her, one arm around her waist, and Anne felt burstingly happy and terrified.

"I'll phone home again in the morning," Carlos remarked just before they stepped back inside, "and we'll see how things stand."

And then we'll agree to stay on a few more days, a few more weeks, forever, Anne thought, and nodded quickly at Carlos, smiling. No matter what the outcome of his phone call, they would surely stay here a day or two longer at least. As she bade everyone good night a few minutes later and went to her bedroom, Anne realized just how much she was counting on those extra days. Here on the Riviera Carlos was warm, relaxed, loving—he was *hers.* When they left here she would lose him again. And she didn't think she could bear it.

Chapter Eight

When Anne saw Carlos again—at breakfast the following morning—every trace of the warmth that had been in his face the previous evening had vanished. His expression was hard and distracted. He had already phoned Palencia, he informed her, and there was still no sign of Dolores or Michael. "Father's becoming more and more upset as each day passes," he told Anne coldly. "It is imperative that we return at once."

Oh, but can't we stay at least one more day? Anne wanted to cry out, but at sight of Carlos's cold black eyes, she bit back the cry. He was right, of course. They'd agreed on a time limit and now must respect it. These three days here had been a delightful dream, nothing more. It was time now to wake up from the dream and once again deal with reality.

They left as soon as possible after breakfast that morning, their suitcases tucked into the trunk of their small rented car, Renée and Bob waving them off with repeated requests that they come again.

"Though next time you won't escape so easily," Renée exclaimed, tears shining in her large green eyes. "Three lousy days. I still can't believe you're really leaving."

"Our days here were anything but lousy," Carlos responded, dark eyes shadowed. "They were beautiful days, and I for one will always remember and be grateful for them." He kissed Renée affectionately on the cheek, shook Bob's hand warmly, then climbed into the little car and started the engine.

Anne crossed her arms over her chest, as though to press to herself the lovely three days they'd had. "Thank you for talking me into this," she murmured after a time to Carlos.

Carlos glanced around with a startled look. Anne could tell he'd heard her voice but had been too far away, in thought, to comprehend what she'd said.

"Nothing," she murmured even more softly, grateful tears glistening in her eyes. "I just wanted to thank you, that's all, for persuading me to come here. It was—well, the most perfect three days of my life, that's all."

"Mine too," Carlos said. His eyes met hers and remained fixed on them for so long that Anne was afraid they'd run off the road.

"Please, Carlos, remember you're driving," she reminded him nervously.

"Right." His steady gaze swung around to the road and he did not glance her way again.

Anne turned to look out her window and almost at once sank into a worried reverie. Why hadn't Michael and Dorrie shown up yet? she wondered. She tried to pretend to herself that she found this more surprising than she actually did. Her brother wasn't a weak man, but neither did he possess the fiery stubbornness that both Dorrie and Carlos possessed in full measure. In the end Michael would win, Anne had no doubt, but it was obviously going to take him a while to bring Dorrie around.

Carlos fell silent as he sped the little car along the highway, and with every mile they drove he seemed to retreat more securely within himself. His face closed up, as though to deny her existence, or at least to deny the enjoyment they had found in each other the past few days. Well, so what? Anne thought, afraid to face the limitless pain this caused her. If Carlos could withdraw emotionally, so could she.

After a time the smoothly rolling car rocked her into drowsiness, and she closed her eyes and fell asleep.

They stopped for a midday meal in Marseilles, and Carlos bought fruit, cheese, and nuts at a market so that they would be able to partake of a light supper later without having to lose any more time. Around midnight they reached Narbonne. Carlos pulled up to a small hotel, announcing that they would rent rooms here. As they bade each other good night, Carlos told Anne coolly that he planned to get an early start in the morning, so if she didn't wake of her own accord, he would come to her room to wake her. Tensing irritably, Anne snapped that she would do her best to awaken on her own.

"Don't blame me for the fact that we're not in Palencia yet," she reminded him. "It wasn't my idea to go off for a three-day holiday, it was yours."

"Admittedly," Carlos replied even more icily, "but now I must return as quickly as possible.

Father's growing more upset by the hour and I'm also needed at my office. It was foolish of me to have taken that time off and now I must pay for it. Good night, Anne."

"Good night, Carlos."

They parted in the hall outside Anne's room. As Anne watched Carlos stride off toward his own room, her eyes misted over and smarted. How could Carlos dismiss the marvelous days they'd had in St. Tropez so easily? He sounded now as though he regretted them, as though he would wish them out of existence if he could. Anne felt suddenly lonely and isolated in a way she'd never felt before. After she went into her room, she lost control and burst into tears. Throwing herself across her bed, she wept, the first time she'd given in to sobs since this whole miserable mess had begun. How could Carlos push out of his mind and heart all memory of their golden days together? Obviously only *she* had enjoyed them; they could not have meant anything at all to him.

In time her sobs ceased and she drifted off to sleep, physically and emotionally exhausted.

When she woke in the morning, she steeled herself not to be hurt by Carlos again. She'd known almost from the moment they met that underneath his handsome, charming façade lived a man who was absolutely ruthless. She had foolishly allowed him to get by her defenses for a time, but not again. Never again would she forget that Carlos, for all his apparent charm, felt nothing for her. There was ample evidence to prove that the man had no heart.

As it turned out, both she and Carlos had

awakened shortly after dawn, and after a quick breakfast they were again on their way. The weather was clear, warm, and beautiful, and much of the scenery they passed was truly spectacular. Nevertheless Anne couldn't seem to relax enough to enjoy their travels. Carlos drove silently hour after hour, eyes staring straight ahead, and every time Anne allowed herself to glance around at him, she felt a fresh wave of anger and pain. She did her best to keep her eyes fixed on the landscape outside her window, and tried desperately to forget that Carlos Philip Maximilian Alvarado-Castellon even existed.

Shortly before noon that day Carlos suddenly swerved the car off the road and stopped. For the first time in hours he addressed her.

"Anne, look up ahead, to the left. I've taken us some distance out of our way, but I couldn't bear to come this close and not let you see Carcassonne, which to me is one of the most fascinating sights not only in France but in all of Europe. Do you not think so?"

With her pulse now racing, Anne squinted her eyes to stare at the walled and towered city ahead, which rose against a background of snowcapped mountain peaks.

"Carcassonne is probably the finest example of a medieval walled city in the world," Carlos told her. "The city itself is said to date back some twenty centuries—can you imagine that, back to the time of Christ?—though the fortifications were built much later, between the thirteenth and fifteenth centuries. As pressed as we are for time, I'd like to stop here just long enough for you to have a closer look.

Maybe we can take a quick tour around the ramparts of the outer wall and catch a bite to eat in the walled town, 'La Cité.' We've made such very good time we can afford to waste an hour or two, don't you think?''

Pulse pounding even harder, Anne glanced around to look directly at Carlos, the first time she had faced him all morning. "It's hard for me to agree or disagree," she said, as calmly as possible, "when I haven't the least idea where we are."

"Then I will have to rectify that situation," Carlos said and smiled. Carcassonne is in the southern-most area of France, nestling, as you can see, at the base of the Pyrences. My idea was this, if it's agree-able to you. We'll explore the town for an hour or so, we'll stop for something to eat, then we'll be on our way again. There are several very passable roads over the mountains, and we can head south to pick one up as soon as we leave Carcassonne."

"If we do that, how soon will we arrive in Palen-cia?"

Carlos smiled. "Whether or not we throw away an hour or two now, we should reach my home by late afternoon tomorrow."

Anne's eyes held his a moment longer, then she lowered her gaze and shrugged slightly. "All right, then. Why not?"

"Good enough." Carlos started the car motor up again and swung the little car back onto the road.

They took the tour of the outer ramparts that Carlos had suggested, strolled through the "lists"—the space between the outer and inner walls—walked through the museum in the Counts' Castle, built in the twelfth century, and spent a brief time going through the Basilica St. Nazaire, gazing with awe at the lovely stained-glass windows built in the thirteenth and fourteenth centuries. After enjoying lunch at a small café in the Lower Town near the Musée des Beaux Arts, they agreed it was time to be once again on their way.

They had talked very little during their sightseeing through Carcassonne, but Anne had sensed that Carlos felt friendlier toward her again. This not only confused her, it also made her angry, and as Carlos sped them on their way she resolved with even greater determination not to let down her guard.

The little car sped smoothly forward. Carlos drove without speaking, his eyes fixed steadily on the road ahead, and again Anne grew drowsy, closed her eyes, and in time fell asleep.

She was awakened suddenly when the car jolted to a stop and Carlos cried out something in Spanish, words that sounded both startled and angry. She jerked upright, saw that it was dark outside, and glanced quickly around at Carlos.

"Carlos, what is it? Why have we stopped?"

"I don't know. I'll have to check." Carlos reached around to the back, grabbed up a flashlight and jacket, and pulled the jacket on before climbing out. He threw up the car hood and his head disappeared under it. Anne sat huddled forward, staring out, aware suddenly that she felt chilled. She rolled down her car window and peered out. The air slapping against her face was clear and cold, and she could see there was snow on the ground just beyond the paved road they were on. She hastily rolled her car window back up, then on impulse climbed out and walked around to stand alongside Carlos.

"Carlos, can I help? Do you know yet what the problem is?"

"Not yet." Carlos glanced around at her, and in the light of the flashlight he held, Anne could see the sudden sparks that flashed in his angry, dark eyes. "But, for heaven's sake, get back in the car. Do you want to freeze? You're not even wearing a coat!"

Yes, master! Anne thought hotly, cheeks flushing with humiliation, but she quickly did as he'd ordered and had to admit to herself that of course he was right.

Headlights came up on the highway behind them and Anne swiveled around on the seat to watch. As the car approached, traveling at a high speed, she suddenly *knew* it would crash into them. A much larger car, it would squash them flat or smack them out of the way as a man would a bug. Tensing in fright, Anne watched in growing panic as the headlights got larger and larger, all but blinding her. But instead of running into them, at the very last minute the car swerved to the side and went roaring past. Though Carlos stood alongside their car waving for the driver to stop, his signal was ignored and the car sped by.

Carlos walked to the driver's door and yanked it open. "Anne, move over behind the wheel," he directed her. "Steer the car while I push it off the road. We're not safe here."

Anne did as he'd asked, hands nervously clasping the wheel. Fortunately the vehicle was small and light enough for one man to move, and soon the little car dipped down into a narrow gully to the side of the road and lurched forward onto some icy ground. Carlos came running up alongside, opened the door and said, breathing fast, "Very good, Anne. The motor has thrown a rod, I'm almost sure, which I have no way to fix, but I'm going to try to stop a car and get us a ride. Bundle up as best you can. Hopefully I won't be long."

A few minutes later another car came speeding by, and about a half hour after that a second. Then there was a long wait before they saw the lights of another car approach and disappear. Although Carlos stood in the middle of the road and waved his flashlight, none of the drivers stopped to help them. Twice he had to make a quick leap aside or he would have been struck. In fear that he would be injured if he didn't give up, Anne rolled down the car window and yelled at him, trying to catch his attention.

When Carlos didn't respond, she climbed out at last in annoyance. Slipping over the icy ground, she made her way over the gully and onto the paved road. Gleaming headlights flashed into view just as she stepped up to Carlos. Waving her arms back and forth, she tried desperately to attract the driver's attention.

"Anne, what the devil—?" Carlos exclaimed, obviously annoyed to see her there.

Ignoring him, Anne continued to signal frantically to the oncoming car. The car swerved to the side, and passed Carlos and herself without even slowing down.

"Anne, go back to the car," Carlos ordered imperiously. "This is no place for a woman to be."

"And no place for a man either!" Anne snapped irritably. "Can't you see you're just wasting your time? No one's going to stop for you. Now come on back to the car before you freeze to death!"

"Here's another car coming now," Carlos responded. "This one will stop for us, I feel it in my heart."

The car raced toward them, swung to the side to avoid them, and roared powerfully on. In spite of herself, Anne burst out laughing.

"In your heart, you said?" she mocked Carlos. "You knew in your heart that car would stop?"

Another car raced past them while they stood in the center of the road ordering each other back to the car. Finally Anne gave up, muttering that if Carlos insisted upon killing himself, all right, so be it. She trudged back to the car alone, and huddled on the front seat trying to warm herself up. Still Carlos stubbornly stayed on the road, frantically flashing his light at the pitifully infrequent cars that passed. Another hour had gone by before he at last gave up and stalked back to the car.

Throwing himself onto the seat, he sighed. "The worst part is I can't even blame those people," he muttered to Anne. "There have been so many cases of robbery, car theft, even murder up on these mountain roads that no driver in his right mind would stop to help anyone. Being a Good Samaritan may be good for the soul but it's highly dangerous to the body, up on these isolated roads, at least. The fact is," he admitted, swinging to face Anne, his black eyes shadowed, "as often as I've traveled this road, I've never once stopped myself for anyone signaling me. I always figure it's a setup, someone out to rob me and take my car. So how can I hold it against anyone else for thinking the same thing and not risking life and limb?"

"I guess we'll have to forget about rescue and just adjust to the idea of spending the night here," she suggested. "Surely we'll be all right. Then in the morning—well, maybe in the morning someone will stop."

"Let's hope so." Carlos reached over to touch Anne's shoulder, smiling. "And thanks for being such a good sport, Anne. I really appreciate it. Be right back."

Again Carlos climbed out of the car. He walked to the rear, opened the trunk, and hauled out their two cases. He tossed them into the back of the car, then climbed in once again behind the wheel.

"It's going to get cold—really cold—so I suggest we put on all the clothes we can, then use what's left to cover ourselves. That way, maybe we'll keep from freezing to death."

"Good idea."

In a friendly, companionable silence they opened their cases and began pulling on additional clothing. Anne grinned as they both began to gain more and more bulk. Carlos grinned in response, and before long, for no particular reason, they both burst out laughing. As their laughter died away, Carlos drew Anne to him and kissed her, his sensuous mouth pressing warmly on hers.

"Anne, you're a truly wonderful girl," he whispered into her ear, then he kissed her ear, her forehead, her cheek, and again her mouth. Never before had he kissed her so gently, with so much tenderness, and in spite of herself Anne felt her body responding, wanting his kiss, the warmth of his arms around her, the fast, hard beating of his heart that she could feel even through all the layers of clothing they wore.

"Oh, Anne, my beautiful, beautiful Anne," Carlos whispered, his breath coming fast, "I want you, Anne. Ever since the first night we met, I've wanted you. And I know you want me too. Don't try to deny it."

Before Anne could answer, could even decide how she wanted to answer, Carlos's mouth again claimed hers. He lifted her awkwardly and slid across the seat under her, so that she sat on his lap away from the steering wheel. As he continued to kiss her, one of his hands went to her throat, then slipped in under the sweater and jacket she wore. Anne felt instantly startled by the warm touch of his fingers. He forced his hand farther down inside her clothing, warm and seeking against her flesh, and Anne felt her own breath coming hard, coming fast. Carlos's arm around her shifted a bit, then again his mouth hungrily sought hers. His exploring hand pushed on, on, and then reached its goal, cupping tightly over her breast.

"Anne, you're so lovely, so warm and lovely," Carlos whispered hoarsely into her ear. "I've tried to ignore the attraction between us, but it is impossible. Oh, Anne, I want you, I want you so much!"

His mouth once again sought hers, passionately pressing it into softness, into openness. His hand drew away from her breast, eased out, pulled her clothing carefully together again, then lowered onto her thigh. His fingers pressed against her outer thigh, through the layers of clothing, molding her slight feminine form to his hard masculine one. His touch seemed to light a fire in her, bringing great warmth, generating an inner, tumultuous warmth that soon had Anne breathing as hard as Carlos, responding to his drugging kisses with all the passion in her, all the mindless passion never before awakened.

"Oh, Carlos," Anne moaned between kisses, and her mind screamed, along with her body, *Oh, darling, don't stop, kiss me, kiss me, love me, and don't ever stop!*

How long they kissed and caressed each other, pressing frantically together in their passion, feeling each other's loving response even through all the bulky clothing they wore, Anne could never afterward estimate. An hour perhaps, or a longer time or a briefer time, who could know? There are moments when time stops, other moments when it stretches out into eternity. All Anne knew for certain later was that they kissed, and Carlos tenderly but passionately caressed her, until time stood still and the universe exploded and the only reality was love. And at last, at last, secure in the arms of love, warmed by the memory of love, the reality of love, she fell asleep, safely cradled in Carlos's arms.

Chapter Nine

Anne woke in the morning feeling stiff and a bit sore but not overly cold. As she glanced around, straightening up, she saw that she was alone in the car. She climbed out, yawning and stretching, and spotted Carlos already up on the highway, signaling frantically to an oncoming car. The car swerved to the side to avoid hitting Carlos, but then about a hundred yards farther on the driver slowed up and stopped.

He rolled down his window and yelled something at Carlos, in Spanish. Carlos called back, and the two engaged in an animated exchange, not a word of which Anne could understand. But Carlos's voice sounded pleased and relieved as he shouted, *"Muchas gracias, señor,"* and he smiled broadly as he waved good-bye to the man.

He ran off the highway and went slipping and sliding down the little gully, his handsome face glowing with light in the clear, cold, early morning air. He came to a stop on the other side of their little car, grinning across at Anne, black eyes flashing with a million stars.

"Buenos días, mi amiga. I do hope you slept

passably well. Certainly you are looking exceedingly pretty this morning, if I may say so."

Anne felt a wave of tension, of annoyance, run through her as she narrowed her eyes and stared across at Carlos. His thick, gleaming black hair had a somewhat tousled look and there was a pleased, knowing smile on his well-formed lips. She had never seen him look more handsome, nor had she ever seen him in what appeared to be such high spirits. Somehow, seeing him like this caused her pain and she instinctively steeled herself against it.

"I slept well enough, thank you," she murmured, her cheeks flushing warmly at the memory of the passionate kisses and tender embraces they had indulged in before falling asleep. "You too, I hope. But what were you and that man saying to each other just now?"

"Oh, that," Carlos responded lightly and laughed. "He agreed to send a tow truck back for us, so we shouldn't be stuck up here for more than an hour or two longer, I hope. With luck we may still make it to my home by tonight, and if not, by tomorrow morning."

Carlos paused for a moment, glancing across at her with dancing black eyes.

"But happily enough, dear Anne, I no longer feel as much pressure as I did before. If we don't make it home until tomorrow or even the day after, so be it. *Que será será.* I had a wonderful dream last night and somehow it still seems so real I no longer worry. Shall I tell you about my dream, or are you Americans far too practical to care about such things?" He grinned teasingly at her, standing on the far side of the little car.

Anne tensed even more painfully. It was almost more than she could endure to continue looking straight across into Carlos's supremely handsome face. *I had a dream last night too,* she thought, the words coming unbidden to her mind; *I dreamed you held me close and kissed me and—*

But *his* dream wouldn't be the same. She knew it wouldn't. She knew hearing it would hurt. She quickly erected as much defense as she could muster and responded casually, "Of course I'd like to hear about your dream if you care to tell me. If not, no matter." She glanced away as casually as possible, with an offhand little shrug.

Carlos burst out laughing. He walked around to her, grabbing hold of her by the arms. His eyes gazed insistently, piercingly down into hers.

"Oh, how nonchalant you Americans are," he said teasingly. "So practical, so pragmatic, pretending you have no romance in your souls, that you have matured beyond foolish romanticism. We Spaniards are the romantics, the mystics, the dreamers, *sí*, while you Americans are all work, science and industry, no? In the face of your yawning indifference, I have half a mind not to tell you of my dream after all."

Stung by his words, by the certainty that what he was about to tell her would hurt as few things had ever hurt her, Anne pulled irritably away, remarking tartly, "Oh, you'll tell me, all right. Obviously you're simply bursting to tell, so don't let me stop you. What was the dream?"

With an air of happy triumph, Carlos leaned forward and kissed Anne's cheek. "Sweet Anne, pretty Anne, lovely Anne," he murmured, "I dreamed that we arrived home and who should come running out to greet me, with a loving smile, throwing her arms around me, but my sister Dolores! The dream was so clear, so very clear. I could see everything, the wide steps, our home in Palencia, and Dolores flying down to meet me with a loving hug and a kiss."

Carlos paused, his smiling eyes gazing down into Anne's. "So now I am sure that all is well. Dolores is already home or soon will be. Father is no longer fretting, worrying himself sick with grief. Now you too, Anne, can relax. In another day, two at most, I will be reunited with my sister and you with your brother. We will both be free of this disastrous affair, you to return home, I to return to my work."

Carlos caught hold of Anne by the shoulders, insistently forcing her to face him again. "Or don't you believe in dreams? Perhaps you think them silly fancies spun by our wishes, with nothing prophetic in them. Is that it, Anne?"

Carlos no longer smiled as he gazed down at her. Rather, his eyes were now shadowed.

Again Anne pulled free. "Who knows?" she answered tartly, stepping away. "Certainly I'm no authority on dreams. Now if you don't mind, I'd rather wait inside the car."

As Anne opened the door to gain her retreat, Carlos walked over to the highway again and began running back and forth along the edge, as though for exercise, to keep himself warm. No sooner was she

123

safely inside the car than stinging tears welled into her eyes. She grabbed a tissue out of her pocket, blew her nose, and composed herself. Obviously last night had meant no more to Carlos than their three golden days in St. Tropez. She kept remembering the interested way he had eyed the voluptuous actresses and models in the restaurant in Paris. Carlos responded to women. From their very first night together, on the boat in Morocco, he had never gone to the least pains to hide this fact. And last night—

Well, obviously he had seen no reason not to take advantage of the situation, no reason not to enjoy a couple of hours of mild lovemaking, of kisses and caresses—what better way to spend the time, under the circumstances? And I certainly can't claim he forced me or harmed me, Anne told herself sternly, trying to ease the terrible pain in her heart, the stunned feeling of betrayal. It wasn't Carlos who had betrayed her, she had to admit. In not resisting him, not mocking him and pushing him away, she had betrayed herself.

A sob of pain burst from her, but she quickly stifled the one that threatened to follow, and again blew her nose. Well, it was all over now, live and learn, she told herself. Carlos had awakened this morning feeling buoyantly happy after his dream, the dream he saw as prophetic. Today or tomorrow they would arrive at his home, Dorrie and Michael would be there, and then Carlos's dear friend Anne would be free to leave, to fly away home—and good riddance to her.

Thanks for being such a good sport, Carlos would

say, and have a nice flight home. Sorry for any inconvenience I may have caused you. Good-bye. Good luck. And away he would go, back to his work, his showgirls, his life. And possibly once every five years for the rest of his life he would remember this dreary affair, the time his beloved sister ran off with that fortune-hunting rascal and for several miserable days he'd been stuck escorting the sister, who fortunately was young and pretty enough and a very good sport.

Ah, yes, a remarkably good sport, allowed me to kiss her whenever the mood arose, didn't seem to mind, never drew the line at anything I wanted, though of course I restrained myself—I'm a gentleman, after all, and had no wish to break the heart of a little American girl, one who had no defenses against me, poor thing. But then her brother brought my sister home again, unharmed and unwed, so that ended that. Wretched affair, but thankfully it ended well, and all's well that ends well, *n'est-ce pas?* Ah, yes.

Stifling another sob, Anne stuffed the damp tissue she'd used down into her jacket pocket and clung to the anger that welled up, nourishing it with all her might. Darn Carlos anyway, who did he think he was? Arrogant son of a duke who felt himself superior to everyone, in particular to Americans. Well, so what? Let him cling to his stupid little illusion of superiority. In another day or two, if his dream turned out to be prophetic, as quite possibly it would, she'd be free of him, free to fly home and push all thought of him out of her mind and out of her heart. Out of her broken, shattered heart.

As she looked toward the highway again, Carlos stopped his running long enough to wave to her. Anne waved listlessly back. A little exercise would probably do her good too, she decided, so she got out of the car, slushed through the narrow gully and climbed up to the edge of the road. Instead of jogging along the road, she began running quickly in place, counting each step. By the time she reached fifty her breath was coming fast and she felt overly warm, burdened by all the clothes she wore. She kept going to a hundred, then forced herself to do twenty more. As she stopped, panting, she unbuttoned her jacket and pulled it off. Carlos came striding up to her, smiling.

"Good for the circulation, yes? Are you as hungry as I am, Anne? I think possibly we might find a cracker or two left over from the other day and maybe even a piece of fruit. Time for breakfast, is it not?"

"All right, if you say so," Anne answered coolly, not smiling in response to Carlos's smile. She swung away and began slushing her way back to the car, feeling a calm sense of triumph, sure now that she would never again succumb, even for a moment, to Carlos's unnerving charm.

It was after eleven before the tow truck finally arrived, by which time they had all but given up hope. They had munched their way through a very meager breakfast, a few nuts and half an apple they'd found in a paper sack in the car. Anne was beginning to feel dizzy and weak from hunger while Carlos insisted, with a laugh, that if they didn't get rescued soon he would take off one of his shoes and, in imitation of Charlie Chaplin, cook it and eat it. Anne smiled coolly in response to this, refusing to feel amused; she wouldn't allow herself to be drawn into friendly conversation. Let Carlos decide she wasn't that good a sport after all. Look where being a good sport last night had gotten her! Never, ever again.

When the tow truck finally arrived, they hooked their little car to its rear and Anne and Carlos climbed into the cab to ride with the driver. As they roared noisily along, Carlos and the driver had several brief but lively bursts of conversation, but as they spoke in Spanish Anne had no idea what they were saying. At one point Carlos, who had his arm along the back of the seat, allowed his hand to drop down onto Anne's shoulder, but she immediately pulled away, annoyed, and Carlos did not again try to touch her. By the time they arrived at the repair shop and climbed back down from the cab of the tow truck, Carlos's expression was coolly withdrawn, and he did not again attempt any show of friendliness.

After they'd dropped off the crippled car, the tow truck drove them a few miles farther to where they could rent another vehicle. They stopped for a delicious hot lunch, and by early afternoon were once again on their way, "no worse for wear," as Carlos put it—though Anne couldn't agree—and only a few hours delayed.

As on the earlier portion of their trip, Carlos rarely spoke while driving. He kept his eyes steadily on the road ahead and seemed to forget he wasn't alone. He would often snap on the car radio, search for music, and hum softly along with the vocalist. Anne spent most of her time staring absently out at the countryside whirling by. Would Michael and Dolores really be there when they arrived at Carlos's home? Sometimes she felt sure they would be— Michael had promised they would—while other times she felt equally sure that Dorrie would prevail. If Michael and Dorrie didn't show up—

Anne's eyes popped open as she found herself suddenly wide awake again. Carlos had agreed to give Michael one week. That week was now up. They'd spent one day driving to the Riviera, three days there, and this was their third day on the journey home—seven days in all. If Carlos stuck by his original plan, he would go to the police immediately if his sister had not returned, and she would be free to leave.

Anne sighed suddenly, wishing that that moment had already arrived, that she was right this minute heading toward an airport to catch a flight home. She had phoned her employer before leaving Paris, explaining that an emergency had arisen and she wanted to extend her vacation for another week. Now that week was up, so if she wanted to hold onto her job she would have to return. If only Michael had won and had dragged Dorrie home!

Oh, that stubborn, willful Dorrie! Anne thought, biting despairingly at her lip. She felt flooded with the certainty that Dolores was every bit as willful, arrogant, selfish, and self-centered as her brother Carlos and might easily never give in. Oh what a mess, Anne thought for the thousandth time, and with another sigh she rested her head back, trying to push all thought of the future out of her mind so that she could drift into forgetful sleep.

When Carlos shook her awake, Anne saw at once it was dark outside. With a shiver of apprehension, she wondered if they had arrived at their destination, but Carlos's words dispelled this notion.

"Anne, I'm feeling dreadfully hungry again, so I've stopped at a restaurant, but I didn't want to leave you alone in the car. Will you join me for dinner?"

Anne felt a spurt of triumph at the coolly formal way in which Carlos addressed her. At least he now understood that their truce was a thing of the past, that she would not tolerate any more casual caresses. "All right, of course," she answered in an equally formal voice. "But how much farther do we have to go?"

"To Palencia, you mean? We've still got about two hundred and sixty kilometers to go. I thought possibly I might be able to make it through without stopping, but I've simply gotten too hungry. Let's go inside."

Although they shared a table for dinner, each might as well have been alone. They both ate steadily, eyes down, and not a single word was exchanged. Anne's sense of triumph grew ever stronger and she told herself she was extremely pleased to have it this way. They were friends no longer, which was the way it should have been all along. Within a few hours they would reach Carlos's home, and if Dolores was there already—oh, please, let her be there already, and Michael, too—Anne told herself she would be delighted to fly home immediately.

After dinner they returned to the car and again Carlos sped them on their way, driving silently, eyes straight ahead. Anne felt increasingly tense as every mile brought them nearer to the moment of truth, the moment when they'd learn whose will had triumphed, Michael's or Dorrie's.

Though she felt wide awake, too worried and upset to let go, Anne in time drifted off into sleep once more. Again she was awakened by Carlos.

"Anne. Anne, wake up, we're here. Wake up, Anne."

Startled, Anne jerked upright, her eyes popping open. Carlos drew back, an arrogant little smile playing around his lips.

"Well, this is it. I'll get our bags and we'll go in. As late as it is, I doubt that my father and aunt will still be up, so we'll go in quietly and wait until morning to introduce you to them." Carlos paused, then added, in a low, mocking tone, "If you have enough energy to make it, that is. If not, I can carry you."

"Of course I can make it," Anne snapped. Throwing open the car door, she climbed out, finding that in spite of her angry words, she did feel a bit wobbly on her feet. Holding on to the car door for a moment, she steadied herself. Carlos moved quickly around to the back of the car, grabbed up their cases, then stepped up behind her.

"Come along, I'll show you the way," he murmured, and Anne, heart suddenly racing wildly, fell into step beside him.

He had stopped the car in a driveway. For the first few steps Anne blinked her eyes repeatedly, trying to adjust them to the darkness. Carlos led the way up some wide stone steps, about twenty of them, then they moved onto a wide stone terrace. From their new vantage point Anne could suddenly see the moon, full and bright in the sky, and as she stared in awe she could make out the outlines of a medieval castle, complete with towers and ramparts, splashed in moonlight. Momentarily she was so overpowered she had to stop to catch her breath. She'd never seen anything quite like this before, not even in the walled city of Carcassonne.

"Oh, Carlos," she exclaimed, "it looks like something out of the Middle Ages!"

In an amused tone, Carlos answered, "It *is* something out of the Middle Ages. Although the castle has been renovated and added to since, it was originally built in 1375 by Carlos Philip, the first duke of Palencia, and my family has lived here ever since."

These words struck almost as much awe in Anne's heart as sight of the moonlit castle had. For the first time she could understand, even sympathize with, the great pride of family Carlos possessed. Imagine knowing not only who all your forebears were, but exactly where they had lived! She and Michael had no knowledge of who their ancestors were beyond their great-grandparents, and she wasn't even sure of all of them. And as for where they had lived—she didn't even know for sure in which house *she* had lived as an infant. She and Michael had lived in a dozen different rented houses as children; as an adult, she had occupied at least six different nondescript apartments. Moving every year or two, from one rental to another, was the story of her life.

In contrast, Carlos had lived in the very same house—house indeed! magnificent castle!—since birth, and before him his family had occupied the same castle for—oh, for centuries. For over six centuries. *If that were true of me, wouldn't I feel I was somebody too?* Anne suddenly asked herself. Of course I would. It made her feel suddenly closer to the man standing beside her, yet at the same time strangely distant from him. More than ever she realized that they were from two different worlds, with an impassable gulf between them. This brought a small lump of sorrow to her throat, but she quickly swallowed it and turned to face Carlos with a smile, the first smile she'd given him all day.

"Well, lead on, Macduff," she said. "Whither thou goest, I will follow."

Flashing her a broad, pleased smile, Carlos began striding forward across the moonlit terrace, leading Anne into his home, into the heart of his pride, into history. Over six hundred years ago this castle had been built. Anne, walking quietly at Carlos's side, felt small, woefully insignificant, yet not unhappily so. Rather, for some reason, for no reason at all, she felt rather proud. What a story this would make to entertain her grandchildren with someday!

Chapter Ten

They stepped through a heavy, beautifully carved, polished wood door into a magnificent entry hall, a room so large and high-ceilinged it took Anne's breath away. To the right was a wide stone stairway, and Carlos led her toward it, walking as lightly and quietly as possible.

"My father's now reached an age," he whispered to her, "where he sleeps very poorly. The slightest noise seems to awaken him. I don't know why that should be because he's seventy-two years old and his hearing is failing, though he's too proud to admit it. Tomorrow when you meet him try to stand on the right side, for his right ear's his good one. He's almost completely deaf on the left."

As they crept quietly up the stairs, Anne whispered back, in surprise, "Your father's seventy-two?" Her own parents, had they still been living, would have been in their mid-fifties. Dorrie had said that Carlos was thirty-one. Anne had imagined their father, the duke, as a man in vigorous middle age.

Carlos glanced around with a small, amused smile. "Yes. He didn't marry until he was forty, which has always seemed to the men of our line the proper age to settle down. I doubt very much that I shall marry before that age."

But you enjoy yourself with long-legged models and voluptuous actresses in the meantime, Anne thought with a touch of scorn. She dropped her eyes, making no further comment.

When they reached the top of the stairs, Carlos motioned her toward the first door on their right. "That's my sister's room," he whispered, a hint of urgency in his voice. "Possibly she has returned since the last time we phoned. I want to check."

As Carlos stepped quietly over to the door, Anne followed on his heels. His hand slid over the door-knob and turned it. He glanced at Anne over his shoulder, frowning. "It's not locked. Dolores always locked it when she retired for the night, but maybe she's gotten less hostile. I'm going to peek in to see."

After noiselessly pushing the door open, Carlos stepped through it, disappearing into the gloom inside. Anne waited in the hall, shivering slightly with apprehension. Within a minute or two, Carlos returned, stepping back into the hall and closing the door.

"The room is empty. No sign of her. Obviously they haven't returned."

As Carlos motioned her to follow him along the wide, high-ceilinged corridor, Anne felt her pulse skip anxiously. She hurried her step to catch up and whispered nervously, "But, Carlos, the week you gave them is already up. Does that mean—will you go to the police tomorrow?"

Carlos stopped walking and faced Anne directly,

his black eyes looking a slight bit startled. "Tomorrow? Well, no, probably not tomorrow."

"Then—you mean you plan to give them a little more time?"

Carlos hesitated before answering. A look of rather embarrassed amusement came into his eyes. He shrugged slightly, smiling. "Yes, I'll give them a bit more time. A few days perhaps, or a week. But come along. The guest room I'm putting you in is right down here."

The room Carlos led her to was warm, spacious, magnificently furnished, by far the most beautiful room Anne had ever slept in. The high ceiling was decorated by an endless variety of cherub faces, each in its own framed square. When Carlos saw her staring up, he told her that though there were over two hundred faces in the ceiling, no two were exactly alike. The high walls were hung with colorful woven tapestries that Carlos mentioned were centuries old and priceless. The furniture was made of solid oak, intricately carved and polished to a lovely sheen.

"This is the French room," Carlos murmured softly with a grin, "which will have to do as we don't have an American room. When the kings of France came here to visit, this is the room in which the queen slept. Tomorrow you'll be able to say that you slept in the bed of French queens."

With a low chuckle, Carlos set her suitcase on the bed and walked quietly back to the polished wood door. He blew her a kiss good night and pulled the heavy door closed.

Anne, still glancing around in awe, could hardly believe her surroundings. She felt almost as though she'd been transported back centuries, into the Middle Ages. Had she really lived in the Middle Ages, she thought rather wryly, she would no doubt have been the lowliest surf, bedding down on filthy straw in an unheated, mud hut. But here in Carlos's home she was being treated like visiting royalty, sleeping in the bed of queens. With a tired but excited grin, she opened the suitcase on her bed and prepared to undress.

In spite of the long hours she had slept while they were traveling, she had barely crawled into bed before she fell fast asleep. Blessed oblivion. A deep sleep in which she was not even bothered by dreams.

She woke very early the next morning and for a time lay still in bed, eyeing the strange and beautiful room. Was the duke awake yet? Was Carlos? With a smile she rolled out of bed and padded barefoot into the adjoining bath. Here was one room that did not confuse her senses, or make her feel she'd been caught up by a time machine and swept back untold centuries. Though the bathroom was a very luxurious one, with fixtures that seemed to be made of black marble and an oversized sunken tub, nevertheless the room was unmistakably modern. Thank goodness, Anne thought, grinning to herself. She was delighted to see that in addition to the sunken tub the room had a stall shower, and reaching in, she turned the hot water faucet on. Imagine living from the day of your birth in a fantastic home such as this one!

After she'd showered and dressed, Anne left her room, opening and closing the heavy, carved door as quietly as possible and all but tiptoeing down the hall toward the stairs. She had no idea what time it was or whether anyone else in the household was up. As she reached the downstairs hall, she ran across a valet in black trousers, white shirt, and black vest.

"Could you tell me whether anyone else is up yet?" she asked him.

He gave her a startled look. *"Perdoneme."* Then a friendly smile broke across his wrinkled old face and he motioned for her to follow him. He led her down the wide hall to where a double open door led into a large high-ceilinged dining room. As she thanked the valet and entered the room, Anne saw that a young woman stood over by a sideboard pouring herself a cup of coffee. The woman was quite tall, with shiny black hair pulled severely into a bun at the back of her neck. She had large dark eyes, thin curved brows, and a spot of high color on each cheek which Anne decided was not natural but rouged on. The woman looked startled as Anne walked in, then forced out a cool, condescending smile.

"Buenos días," she murmured. *"Bienvenido."*

"Thank you," Anne murmured in embarrassment, feeling her cheeks flush warmly. *"Buenos días* to you too."

"Oh, you're an American," the young woman said, in a faintly contemptuous tone. "You arrived here last night with Carlos, did you not? I'm Maria Carlotta Isabel Domingo-Almazan, a very close family friend. Would you like some coffee?"

"Yes, thank you, I'd love some. I'm Anne McCullough."

"And how do you take your coffee?"

"Just black, thank you."

Maria picked up a cup from the sideboard, poured Anne a cup, and handed it to her, dark eyes narrowed as they insistently surveyed her. "You did arrive here with Carlos last night, did you not?"

"Oh, yes. Yes, I did," Anne answered quickly, fearful that she'd been rude by not affirming this when Maria first asked.

"Shall we sit down?" Maria suggested. "I've already ordered breakfast and it should arrive very soon. You've been traveling with Carlos, have you?" Maria tried, it seemed to Anne, to ask this as casually as possible, to mask an intense interest she apparently had.

Anne felt her cheeks flush even more warmly. As Maria sank down on one of the high-backed chairs at the long, highly polished, gleaming table, Anne rather reluctantly sat down on an adjoining chair. She hadn't expected to be met with a grilling this early in the morning, at least not by some young woman whose relationship to Carlos's family she could not grasp. Carlos had repeatedly mentioned his father and aunt but never a single word that Anne could remember about any Maria Carlotta Whatever-it-was. Had Maria heard about Dorrie's running away or was that being kept a family secret? Maria had said she was a very close family friend—how close did that mean?

"Well, yes, I have been traveling with him," Anne murmured nervously after taking a bracing sip of the steaming hot, delicious coffee. She started to add

138

that after leaving Paris they'd spent a few days on the Riviera but then thought better of it. Again she sipped at her coffee, saying nothing more.

"And are you an actress or something?" Maria asked a moment later, in a distinctly annoyed, impatient voice. Her thin, black brows almost drew together over her narrow-bridged, sharp nose as she gazed irritably over her coffee cup at Anne. *The poor woman can't figure me out, can't decide who I am, how I fit in,* Anne thought with a sudden spurt of amusement, *any more than I can figure out who she is.* This thought made her feel a great deal more in control and she lifted her eyes to meet Maria's with a small, friendly smile.

"Well, I don't know exactly what you mean by 'or something,'" she murmured, "but, no, I most certainly am not an actress. Back home in Baltimore, in the States, I work in a bank. I'm a teller. It's a dignified, respectable job but not very exciting, I'm afraid."

As Anne sipped her coffee again, so did Maria. "Then you're over here on vacation?" Maria demanded next, with open impatience. Though she sat gazing directly across at Anne, Anne still received the impression that this haughty young woman was looking down her sharp nose at her. She began to feel more than a little annoyed. And what possible business is that of yours? she wanted to answer.

Instead she merely nodded, glancing away, trying to avoid any further conversation.

Maria gulped down the last of her coffee, rose, and walked irritably over to the sideboard to refill her cup. "And you met Carlos on the Riviera, did you?" she asked next, acting thoroughly exasperated that she was having such a time extracting information from this uncooperative young commoner.

Anne felt a little smile pull on her mouth as she sipped her coffee again and took her own good time to answer. "Well, no, as a matter of fact I didn't," she murmured at last, offering nothing further.

Before Maria had a chance to pursue her questioning, steps could be heard in the hall outside and Carlos came striding into the room. As Anne glanced around to welcome him, she felt her heart leap painfully at how impossibly handsome he looked. Whenever she saw him after a lapse of time she was again astonished that any face could be so charmingly attractive, any form so lean and masculine. Carlos was elegantly yet quite casually dressed in black slacks and a light blue silk shirt, open at the neck. The blue of the shirt made his thick black hair seem even blacker. His dark eyes lit with surprise—and pleasure?—as he saw Maria and he walked quickly to her, pressing a kiss on her cheek.

"Maria," he murmured, followed by a stream of mellifluous Spanish. He had reached for Maria's hand and held it as he spoke. A moment later he turned around and noticed Anne. "Well, Anne, good morning," he said in a buoyant voice, with a quick warm smile. "So you awakened before I did. You've met Maria, I presume? What a surprise, and pleasure, to find you here. She's a very dear family friend, as possibly she mentioned."

"Yes," Anne agreed, nodding.

"And why wouldn't I have come?" Maria protested in a decidedly petulant tone. "At a time of crisis like this, of course I rushed here to offer what comfort I could. Your poor father—your aunt— Have you the least notion, dear Carlos, how worried they are, how distraught? While you have been sunning yourself on the Riviera, frolicking with your friends"—as she said this, Maria glanced resentfully over at Anne—"*I* have spent *my* days holding your poor aunt's hand, trying to get her to dry her tears. And as for your father—oh, how difficult it was to comfort him! He wanted *you* here, Carlos, he wants his beloved little Dolores back. Can you not at least imagine how it tears at the poor man's heart to fear for the safety, the very life, of his only daughter? He *needed* you, Carlos, yet where were you? Why did you not speed directly home from Paris?"

"Because I did not, that's all," Carlos responded in a tone so nonchalant Anne could scarcely believe her ears. He poured himself coffee and walked over to take a chair at the head of the table, a few feet from where Anne sat, and to Anne's even greater surprise he threw her a wink. "I told father over the phone that Dolores was perfectly all right, that there was not the least need to fear for her safety much less her life. The moment I see him this morning, I shall reassure him of this again."

"And how do you know that?" Maria cried, obviously offended by Carlos's rather casual confidence. "How do you know she's not being threatened, tortured, or raped?"

In spite of herself, Anne burst out laughing at

141

Maria's melodramatic speech. Carlos grinned broadly and again winked at Anne.

"Bring your coffee over and join us," Carlos suggested. "Sit down and calm down, please. I spoke to Dolores over the phone, as I told father when I called, and she sounded fine. More than fine. Full of spirit and stubbornness. Anything but frightened and crushed, believe me."

The spots of color on Maria's cheeks suddenly looked even brighter. "And how do you know she wasn't being forced to say what she said to you? How do you know her kidnapper didn't hold a knife at her throat or a gun at her head? You spoke to her over the phone, indeed! What does that mean?"

"Please, Maria," Carlos answered patiently. "Do sit down and drink your coffee. In the first place, Dolores wasn't *kidnapped* in the sense you're claiming. She ran away with this man of her own free will. And as I explained to father, we now have a way to pry her loose and bring her back without our having to chase after them. When I had gotten the situation under control, I decided to enjoy a few days off, the first real vacation I've had in years. Thank you for being here with my father and aunt, but now that I am back you need not concern yourself over them. Everything's going to work out fine."

"Just the same," Maria insisted, "I intend to honor your aunt's request to stay until this matter is finally settled." An aggrieved expression on her face, she sipped sulkily at her coffee, eyes lowered.

The sound of steps interrupted the brief silence, and glancing quickly around Anne saw an elderly man and woman enter the room. The man, who had to be Carlos's father, had a thin, stern face with a neatly trimmed, gray-streaked, Vandyke beard. His thick gray hair was combed straight back from his high forehead. He had a narrow, aristocratic nose, fine, firm lips, an extremely erect posture, and seemed wrapped up in an impenetrable, imperious air. As Anne watched him walk in, she felt once again swept back in time, as she had the night before upon entering this castle. Here was a man who surely belonged to the Middle Ages, whose portrait she had glimpsed a hundred times in art museums, the perfect owner of this castle, a man who looked every inch the Spanish nobleman he was.

The gray-haired woman who walked at his side was also quite tall, extremely erect of posture, with a pale skin remarkably wrinkle-free. At first glance Anne felt sure the woman had been as beautiful in her youth as her niece Dolores was now. Again Anne felt that she now understood Carlos and his family much better. Unlike nondescript people like Michael and herself, these people had a name, a heritage, a tradition to uphold. They *were* tradition. And she and Michael were ignorant upstarts trying to push their way into a proud, settled way of life where they weren't wanted and didn't belong. If Michael had any pride, he'd return Dolores to her family and drop out of her life. And if *I* had any pride, Anne thought, with a sudden wave of pain, I'd push Carlos out of my heart once and for all!

"Father, how well you're looking." Carlos jumped up, smiling, and walked over to greet the elderly

143

man. He pressed a quick kiss on his father's cheek, then turned to the woman. "And Aunt Isabel, you're looking well too, as radiantly beautiful as ever." He kissed her on the brow and momentarily put his arm across her shoulder to give her a hug. "Maria's already here, as you can see, but come meet my friend, Anne, who arrived with me during the night."

The trio stopped a few feet from where Anne sat, and Anne rose nervously to her feet, doing her best to face these imposing aristocrats without cringing or crumbling.

"Aunt Isabel, father, this is Anne McCullough. Anne, my father, Philip Frederico Diego Alvarado, duke of Palencia, and his sister, Isabel Dona Teresa Alvarado."

"How do you do?" Anne's cheeks flushed with embarrassment as she wondered how one addressed people such as this. Certainly not by their first names. But—how?

"To meet you is our very great pleasure indeed," Carlos's father greeted Anne gallantly, offering her a very slight bow. His stern old face broke into a small, pleasant smile. "Possibly you are an acquaintance of Carlos's American friends with whom he has recently spent a few days on the French Riviera, is that so?" One of the duke's brows lifted rather quizzically as he awaited Anne's confirmation.

"Well, no, I'm not," Anne murmured tensely, her cheeks flushing even more warmly.

Carlos smiled at her reaction. "No, father, that's a good guess but an incorrect one. Anne was with me on the Riviera, but we didn't meet there. The fact is we met in Morocco, then again in Paris, and have been traveling together ever since. I mentioned her name, father, but possibly you did not catch it. This is Anne McCullough, the sister of the young man with whom Dolores is presently traveling, Michael McCullough."

"The sister—" The old man echoed this softly as though in shock. Carlos's Aunt Isabel, who had been standing beside her brother smiling pleasantly, stiffened at once, drawing herself up even more rigidly. As though of one accord, the elderly pair backed away from Anne, both of them eyeing her with instant distaste.

A moment later the duke's eyes drew away and from then on it was as though Anne no longer existed, or at any rate was no longer present in the room. "And why did you bring such a person here?" Duke Philip demanded of his son. "I don't understand this, Carlos. Explain yourself. What is the sister of that thief and scoundrel doing here? And why has not Dolores returned as you have repeatedly assured me that she would? Your only sister is in dire jeopardy, yet first you take off on holiday to enjoy yourself on the Riviera and now you arrive home with this—this person who most assuredly does not belong here. I cannot fathom your behavior in this matter and demand that you explain, right this moment."

Before Carlos had a chance to reply, the duke's elderly sister addressed her nephew in Spanish, Maria jumped up and joined in the attack, and when

Carlos finally got a chance to speak he too spoke in Spanish. Anne stood by the table in acute embarrassment, her dry mouth aching for a sip or two more of coffee, while she felt too uncomfortable to reseat herself or reach for her cup. She was afraid that if she tried to lift her cup she was so nervous she might easily spill the coffee. *And that's all I need*, Anne thought, lowering her glance as a small, unhappy smile twitched along her lips.

As the family argument continued to rage in a language she couldn't understand, with no one even glancing her way, Anne decided her best course of action was to leave the room as quietly and unobtrusively as possible. She stepped away from the table and walked quickly toward the exit. Just as she reached the open double doors into the hall, her nostrils were assailed by the delectable odor of hot food being carried in on trays. Anne suddenly felt so hungry she almost turned back, drawn by the delightful aroma of what would assuredly be deliciously appetizing food. But her embarrassment proved even stronger than her hunger and she exited quickly from the room, walking hurriedly away down the hall. It wasn't until she reached the front entry that she was out of earshot of the heated family argument being carried on in Spanish.

Because she could think of nowhere else to go, Anne went upstairs to the room in which she had slept. Sighing, she packed everything she had taken from her suitcase the night before, then carefully tidied the room, trying to erase every scrap of evidence that she had ever been there. She was in the bathroom, carefully washing the black marble basin, when she heard a loud rapping on her bedroom door. The next moment the door opened and the elderly valet she'd met downstairs stepped into the room.

He carried a tray upon which sat various covered dishes. The escaping aroma of the food reminded Anne of just how hungry she was. Smiling in delight, she walked over to the valet, murmuring, *"Gracias, gracias,"* and took the tray from him. After a careful survey of the room, she spread a towel on the magnificent chest at the foot of the bed, sat down on one end and spread out her breakfast feast before her. And a feast it was: orange juice that tasted freshly squeezed, toast, butter, strawberry jam, six slices of crisply fried bacon, scrambled eggs, a sweet roll, a bowl of oatmeal with sugar and cream, and an ample supply of coffee. Anne dove in with relish and surprised herself by eating every bite. Carlos's family not only had a beautiful home in which to live, they obviously had an excellent household staff, and, best of all, a most efficient and marvelous cook. How one's outlook on life could improve with a hearty, delicious meal like that one!

After downing the last sip of coffee, Anne decided to leave her room and venture downstairs. Possibly Carlos and his family had resolved their differences by now and Carlos would inform her that, as she was most definitely *persona non grata* here, she was free to leave. Failing that, maybe Michael and Dorrie would show up today. Yes, Anne thought, feeling unreasonably happy and optimistic as she descended the stairs, surely they would arrive today. And once they had—

Anne sighed. Well, who knew what the outcome would be once they arrived? Would Dorrie and Michael be able to persuade her family that he was not a thief and scoundrel after all but Dorrie's one true love, and that the two of them were determined to marry? Would Dorrie's elderly father relent and give the young lovers his blessing?

But no matter what the outcome, Anne thought suddenly, her head suddenly aching, she would be leaving Carlos forever. Michael's chances of winding up happily married to Dorrie might be very slight, but at least some slight chance did exist, while her own chances of winning Carlos were absolutely nil. It was idiotic even to allow herself to think of him that way. She could see that even more clearly now that she was here in his home, and had met his father, aunt, and good friend Maria. Anne's head suddenly ached even more keenly. Who was Maria anyway?

As she reached the downstairs hall, Anne saw in dismay that the object of her thoughts was rapidly approaching her.

"Well, hello, again," Maria greeted her with cool condescension. "Weren't you hungry? You walked out earlier just as breakfast was being brought in. I'm looking for my fiancé. I don't suppose you've seen him?"

Anne felt something heavy and cold drop down through her. "Your fiancé?" she echoed. "Carlos, you mean?"

"Of course Carlos!" Maria snapped, with a look that said, *Who else could it be, you idiot?* "He left the dining room a very short time ago and seems to have disappeared. If you happen to run across him, you might mention that I am looking for him." Maria swung away and began ascending the wide stone stairs.

Anne stood in the hall staring up after the departing woman. So—that's who Maria was. Carlos's fiancée. He could at least have told me, Anne thought sickly, then immediately scolded herself for daring to imagine that it was any concern of hers. Dorrie had warned her that very first day that while Carlos might become involved in any number of romances, he would never marry a woman who wasn't his social equal. Maria apparently was. And no matter how her heart might ache, it was absolutely no concern of hers.

Seeing no one else around, Anne decided to go outside for a walk. After she'd pulled open the heavy carved door and stepped through it, she saw to her surprise that Carlos was striding energetically up the wide steps to where she stood. Her heart caught in pain at sight of him, his aristocratic face unfairly handsome in the midmorning light. As he caught sight of her, a smile curved his well-formed lips.

Reaching her side, Carlos took hold of her arm. "Well, I've been looking everywhere for you. When you left the dining room earlier, I thought maybe you'd been offended."

"And why would I have been offended?" Anne

jerked her arm free of Carlos's hold and glanced angrily at him. After all, he was the one to blame for dragging her here and thrusting her into this totally impossible situation.

Carlos's black eyes fixed on hers and in response to her obvious anger, he grinned even more broadly. "All right, all right," he murmured placatingly, "I know you were not treated with the greatest courtesy and I apologize for that, but try to see it from my family's point of view, please. In any case, let's forget it for now and go for a walk. I'd like to show you the gardens and the view."

"But your fiancée's looking for you," Anne snapped tartly. "She asked me to tell you if I happened to see you."

"My fiancée?" A puzzled look appeared momentarily in Carlos's eyes, then disappeared almost as quickly as it had come. "Oh, Maria, you mean. We'll have to postpone our walk then, but if you'll wait for me here, please, Anne—"

"You didn't tell me you were engaged!" Anne snapped with even more obvious anger, her blue eyes spitting fury.

Carlos had taken a step away, but he turned back at once, again looking surprised. As his eyes met Anne's candidly, he shrugged. "But we're not formally engaged yet," he responded matter-of-factly. "That Maria would even refer to me as her fiancé surprises me. I never refer to her that way."

"But—are you engaged or aren't you?" Anne demanded, her pulse pounding hard. She told herself scornfully she had no right to ask—and no possible interest in Carlos's answer—even as she spoke these words.

Again Carlos shrugged, his grin vanished, his expression growing increasingly guarded. "In a way, yes. In another way, no. From the day Maria was born it was agreed upon by our families that one day we would marry. I've always known this. Maria has always known it. In that sense we are already betrothed. At the same time, as I explained to you last night, I do not expect to marry for several years yet, possibly, like my father, not until I am forty. So why should we become formally engaged so many years before we intend to marry?"

"And meanwhile," Anne lashed out with uncontrollable anger, "you enjoy yourself with an endless string of actresses and showgirls, right?"

Carlos's face broke into a broad, surprised grin. "Showgirls and actresses? Wherever did you get that idea? Obviously you are confusing me with someone else, maybe the hero or villain of some movie you have seen. I'm a hardworking businessman, not a playboy. Ah, you Americans," he ended, shaking his head in deep amusement.

"Confusing you with someone else indeed!" Anne flared furiously. "I saw how you eyed all those long-legged, painted, voluptuous women at the café you took me to in Paris. And the very first thing Maria asked me was whether I was an actress, proving she knows you all right, just as I do!"

"She asked if you were an actress?" Carlos asked incredulously, then he burst out laughing, as though the idea amused him beyond words. "An actress?

151

Oh, good heavens, couldn't she take one look at you and see that you aren't? An actress, indeed!"

Carlos laughed again, almost as heartily, while Anne's cheeks flushed crimson. Was Carlos defending her against an insult Maria had thrown at her, or insulting her himself? She didn't know. She only knew she felt furious, angrier than she'd ever been in her life.

"And as for that café we went to," Carlos added as his new burst of laughter died away, "have I not as much right as other men to look and enjoy? Does this make me a playboy? Certainly I enjoy looking at pretty women, actresses or not, showgirls or not. From the first night we met I have mentioned that you, Anne McCullough, are an extremely pretty girl, so I enjoy looking at you. If a man is to be condemned for that, how many would be left alive in this world, eh, tell me that?"

Anne's blue eyes glared even more furiously into Carlos's amused black ones. *And what of all the kisses, the embraces, all the soft words?* she thought wildly, with terrible hurt. But those were her responsibility as much as his; she had allowed them. Having allowed them to happen, she had no right to reproach him now. Yet the pain was there, and she couldn't seem to push it away.

"Well, your fiancée's still looking for you," she muttered, "and you shouldn't keep her waiting any longer." She swung her eyes away and began running down the steps. "And while you're talking with her, I'll go have a look at the gardens myself."

"But—Anne, why don't you wait? You'll need a guide," Carlos called after her, his voice serious now.

"Nonsense!" Anne called back, not glancing around. "I'm sure I'll do fine." *Once I can make the pain of loving you go away—if I ever can.*

Chapter Eleven

Two days passed with no sign of Michael. The third day dawned and Anne woke with a burning anger, an anger that had grown hourly since her arrival here. It wasn't that she was actively mistreated; she wasn't. At the same time she was miserably aware that she wasn't welcome, that she was barely tolerated. After that first flareup in her presence when Carlos's father and aunt had learned who she was, they had not again, either one, been openly unpleasant to her. Rather, they neglected to speak to her at all. If she happened to run across them in the upper or lower hall, they would not even bother to avert their eyes; they would simply look right through her.

Maria, on the other hand, looked right at her, spoke to her, even occasionally smiled at her, all with the coldest, most sneering condescension imaginable. *Oh, I hate this place!* Anne thought. She felt angry not only at Carlos for bringing her here, at his family for despising her, at Maria for being the woman she was—a self-centered, unpleasant, incurable snob—she also felt angry at her brother, at Dolores, at the world. Where was Michael anyway?

After lying in bed for quite some time staring up at all those round cherub faces carved into the ceiling, carvings she'd found charming at first sight but which by now she'd grown to loathe, Anne dragged herself out of bed and into her luxurious black marble bathroom to shower. She had slept as late as she could manage and her breakfast would be arriving any time, brought by the elderly valet who seemed to be her one and only friend here. But as the man apparently understood not a word of English, and her Spanish was limited to *buenos días, buenas noches,* and *gracias,* they really couldn't communicate too well. Still she sensed that the sweet old man was concerned for her and it made her feel just a slight bit less lonely, a slight bit less trapped. Oh, if only Michael would keep his word and show up with Dorrie!

During the two days just past Anne had had her breakfast in her room alone each morning, her lunch at a table in the rose garden, also alone, but for dinner the kindly old valet had led her each evening to the dining room where the others sat at the table, waiting for her. Only at dinner had she seen Carlos, who had returned to work in the nearby city of Palencia and was gone all day. The first evening when she'd walked toward the table, trembling slightly, wondering how she'd be greeted, Carlos had risen at once at her entrance and smiled warmly at her.

"Well, Anne, how nice to see you. I hope your day was pleasant enough. Will you sit here, please?"

Carlos walked around the table to help her into the chair alongside Maria. Across from them sat

Carlos's aunt, while his father was seated at one end of the table, Carlos at the other. Anne noticed that the elderly duke had also risen at her entrance, but he did not otherwise acknowledge her presence. With his narrow face sternly impassive, he seated himself as Anne sat down. It seemed to Anne that the chill in the air was so marked, so oppressive, that they might all suffer frostbite if they lingered over their dinner too long.

The meal was served in several courses, by two quietly efficient waiters. As they were consuming their first course, a thick, delicious soup, Carlos tried to initiate conversation. He spoke briefly to his father about company matters, politely inquired of his aunt how she was feeling, asked Maria how she had occupied herself while he was gone, and facing Anne, smiling, asked her whether she was enjoying herself. No one answered his inquiries in more than a few brief words, and Carlos's attempts to force further conversation fell flat. Before long Carlos, with a sigh, gave up and turned his attention to the food, which was excellent. Anne, however, felt too angry and uncomfortable to enjoy a single bite she ate. She couldn't wait to be done with the meal so she could leave the room and be free of these insufferable people.

As the dessert was brought in, Anne murmured that she didn't care for any and asked to be excused. Without waiting for permission to leave—she was no child to *need* permission!—she pushed her chair back, stood up, and hurried out of the room.

She started up the stairs, then on second thought swung around and let herself out through the massive front door. During the day she had explored the area surrounding the castle and was now familiar with the various gardens, garages, tennis courts, and greenhouses. Relieved to be alone, she walked through the lovely cool of the evening and told herself a hundred times that Michael would arrive the following day with Dorrie, and she would pack and fly home. And what a relief that would be!

But Michael didn't arrive the next day, nor phone, and Anne found herself growing ever angrier, ever more ready to explode. The day seemed endless. In spite of the lovely gardens where she spent hours strolling, she felt lonely, restless, stiflingly bored. In the late afternoon she saw Carlos's black Mercedes come speeding up the road and she felt her pulse give a happy leap. So hungry was she for companionship she almost headed toward the garage to intercept him. But almost at once she remembered the intense anger she felt toward him, and the million and one times she had vowed to herself to forget him. So instead of heading down to greet him, she swung around and hurried inside, breaking into a run up the stairs so that she would reach her room, and safety, before he had any chance to stop her.

Dinner that night was a rerun of the evening before, with the air even icier, if possible. Even Carlos remained quiet, his dark eyes down as he ate, as though he now realized the futility of trying to enliven the meal with conversation. Again Anne excused herself early and hurried outside to go for a walk. Sometime later, as she was walking back to the castle, she saw Carlos step outside. He stood on the terrace for some time, frowning, glancing around, then he walked thoughtfully down the wide steps. Anne's pulse suddenly raced as she became convinced that he had come out here looking for her. The thought sent a spurt of pleasure through her, yet she felt instantly determined, perversely, to make sure that he did not find her. Like a child playing hide-and-seek, she hid herself behind a massive statue in the rose garden until Carlos had walked by and she could slip behind him into the castle without being seen. If he wanted company for his after-dinner stroll, let him walk with his fiancée!

Once she was safely back in her room, alone, Anne began to feel restless and lonely again and half regretted that she hadn't allowed Carlos to find her, or hadn't walked out to greet him of her own free will. But loneliness is better than pain, she persuaded herself. If she had any sense at all, she would avoid Carlos as much as humanly possible until she was at last entirely free of him.

As she lay in bed that third morning, Anne finally came to a decision. If Michael did not return today, she would leave anyway, regardless of the situation that would leave him in. He was her one and only brother, but the sacrifices she would make for him had to have a limit. Surely she had already done more than he'd had any right to expect. He knew the circumstances she was in, had acted outraged, had insisted he would come save her at once—yet here she languished, in this vile cold prison, waiting, waiting, waiting. *Michael, if you don't come today, I've got to leave. Even if Carlos goes to the police and the police catch you and throw you in jail! Why should I rot in prison instead of you? I've been a prisoner long enough—it's your turn now!*

This is what Anne vowed to herself as she showered, dressed, listlessly ate the breakfast her friend the valet brought, and left her room to wander downstairs to somehow get through another long day. *My very last day here,* she told herself; *this is it, this is it.* But even as she thought this, she clung fiercely to the belief that Michael would show up.

Evening fell, however, and there was still no sign of either Michael or Carlos's stubborn, selfish, self-centered sister.

To avoid running across Carlos after his return from work, Anne climbed the stairs to her room early that evening and threw herself restlessly, miserably, across her bed. For two nights she had gone downstairs for dinner to be treated with icy disdain, as a cold silence enveloped the table. Tonight she wouldn't go down; she'd have her dinner alone here in her room. Or if her friend the valet didn't bring her anything, she would go without, which was all right too.

When the elderly valet rapped softly on her door, then opened it to beckon her to follow him, Anne raised herself to a sitting position on her bed and shook her head. She repeated the word, "No," several times; then, because the sweet old man looked so perturbed, she pressed her hand against her abdomen and made an unhappy face, as though she preferred not to go down to dinner due to a digestive problem. At last the old man seemed to understand, and throwing her a sympathetic glance, backed out of the room again and closed the door.

Within minutes there was another knock on the door, sharp and presumptuous. "Anne, this is Carlos. May I come in?"

Anne, who had flopped restlessly back down on the bed after the valet's departure, instantly swung up to a sitting position. Her pulse raced. She had never supposed Carlos would come after her. "Go away," she called in a clear, cold voice.

"I want to talk to you, Anne," Carlos spoke quietly, calmly. "I've got important news for you. I heard from Michael today."

As she heard these words, Anne's pulse seemed to stop, then the next instant it raced furiously again. She jumped off the bed and stood alongside it nervously biting her lip. At last she called back, "Carlos, I don't believe you. Just go away, please."

"Anne, will you kindly behave yourself? Michael phoned me today. Besides that, Pedro said you were ill. Are you ill?"

"No, I'm not ill! And I still don't believe you. Please go away."

There was silence for a moment, for such a long moment that Anne half believed—feared?—that Carlos had taken her at her word and left. But then the door opened and Carlos stood in the doorway, black eyes glaring at her.

"I'm not in the habit of entering a lady's bedchamber without invitation," he muttered angrily, "but when I'm up against a girl as stubborn and self-willed as you are, what choice do I have? Michael phoned me late this afternoon at the office. He said he was in Tangier. He is on his way and will catch the ferry to Algeciras in the morning. He should arrive tomorrow night or the following morning. He wanted me to tell you and to ask you to forgive him for not coming before now. He realizes that you may be so angry at him by now that you won't believe anything he says, but he wants you to know he feels dreadfully guilty and upset. He tried to phone you here at the castle but we have an unlisted number and Dolores refused to give it to him." Carlos paused momentarily, then added, with a little smile that somehow looked both terribly sad and a little smug, "They are not speaking to each other at present, have split up, as you Americans put it, and no longer plan to marry. So much for the wonderful romantic love they shared that you tried to tell me would last forever."

"Oh, no!" Anne sank down to sit on the bed, feeling terribly shaken. "Then Dolores—?"

"Dolores came on the line to tell me that regardless of what Michael does she hates me, hates our father, hates everything about our life, and is not coming back. Ever, she said. She has the jewels, a forged passport, and is flying to America, she says, to start a new life without even your brother, whom she now claims to hate. He has betrayed their love, betrayed her, according to my highly dramatic, self-willed young sister. So that's how it stands."

Anne's eyes felt suddenly sore and hurting as she stared at him. "But—if Michael comes here without Dolores—?"

Carlos shrugged, then glanced away. "He said he was ready to report to the nearest police station and to tell them to go ahead and arrest him if this will immediately free you to fly home. He is not afraid to be charged with theft, he says, for he knows he is innocent. On top of that, now that he has lost Dolores he does not care in the least what happens to him. His only worry is for you. That was the message he wanted me to give you."

"Oh, no!" Anne felt tears pressing suddenly against her eyelids. What a mess! All because two impetuous young people had decided they loved each other so much that nothing else mattered. And now they weren't even speaking to one another.

"Well, thank you, Carlos, for letting me know," Anne murmured a moment later. "And I'm sorry I was so stubborn about inviting you in. I thought you'd come simply to fetch me for dinner."

Carlos's black eyes swung quickly around to fasten on her. "I did come for that, too. Dinner is ready to be served and is being held up solely because you have not yet consented to join us. You are keeping everyone waiting, and as your host I insist you come this minute to join us."

Carlos's coolly imperious tone immediately awakened the anger that had been sleeping inside her all day. She jumped up and glared at him.

"Well, insist all you like. I'm not coming. And don't suddenly throw manners at me. You did not invite me to come here, you *forced* me to. You're not my host, you're my jailer!"

"All right," Carlos snapped in answer, sounding as angry as Anne felt, "then as your jailer I order you to dine with me. Now come along." He took several long strides forward and grabbed Anne by one wrist, as though to force her if she resisted.

In an instant fury, Anne jerked her arm free.

"And if I won't? If I won't obey? What will you do then, your lordship? Shoot me?"

Carlos again grabbed for her wrist, in his fury gripping it with bruising strength. "No, I won't shoot you. But very possibly I'll pick you up and carry you, if necessary."

Anne tried to jerk her arm free again, without success. Carlos held on too tightly. Breathing hard, she snapped, "And if you do, I'll scream every step. Believe me, I will. Just who do you think you are?"

Carlos's black eyes glared furiously into hers. "You've just told me who I am," he said, his breath coming hard and fast. "Your jailer. Your enemy. A man who is sick to death of the roller-coaster ride you've been putting him through."

The next moment Carlos stepped even closer, pulled Anne against him, and his angry mouth came down on hers, almost painfully hard, more passionately possessive than ever before. Carlos's arms went around her and he held her pressed furiously against him, his mouth capturing hers, possessing hers. Anne found herself almost unable to breathe. Her heart beat so fast it frightened her. She wanted to break free, wanted to cry out, but instead she found herself responding to the dizzying passion in his kiss. Then a moment later Carlos let her loose again and backed off.

"All right, you stubborn little fool, if you don't want to join us for dinner, then don't." He spun on his heel and left her room.

Anne stared after him with hot, hurting eyes, then a moment later threw herself down on her bed. Oh, what a wretched life this was! But Michael would be here by tomorrow night and she would, at long last, be free.

When Anne awoke the next morning she was immediately aware that her anger had drained away and that life once again was good. She felt patient, relaxed and happy in a way she hadn't since her first morning here. After a delicious hot breakfast in her room, brought by her friend the valet, she went downstairs and out of the castle to spend her day in the gardens again. Reminding herself that this would be her last opportunity to enjoy them, she absorbed the lovely sights and bewitching odors with a joyful nostalgia. By nightfall Michael would arrive; tomorrow this enchanted place would be only a memory.

But night fell with still no sign of her brother. Anne again resolved not to join Carlos and his family for dinner, and this evening Carlos did not come to her room to try to drag her downstairs. For a time Anne, isolated in her room, beginning to feel very hungry, worried that she'd been forgotten. It seemed her one friend in the entire castle, the elderly valet, was not going to bring her anything to eat. But just as she was beginning to feel sadly mistreated there was a gentle rap on her door and in came her friend bearing a large silver tray laden with dishes. Surely, Anne told herself as she settled down before the aromatic tray of food, Michael would arrive before she finished eating.

But he didn't, and he still hadn't arrived some two hours later when Anne, weary of waiting, finally undressed, climbed into bed, and tried to sleep.

Anne felt anxious and impatient from the moment she woke the next day, her fifth in Carlos's home. She showered, dressed, and left her room before her friend the valet had even brought her breakfast. For the first time in days she ventured into the dining room, hoping to find Maria. But there was no sign of Carlos's fiancée or of anyone else. She helped herself to a cup of hot coffee, which she sipped impatiently as she waited tensely at the table, but though she remained in the room for quite some time, no one appeared. Nor did any food arrive.

Feeling far more worried than hungry, Anne left the dining room and went outside. There she sat on the wide stone steps, watching for Michael. She spent most of the morning there, in the hot sun, playing a waiting game. Around eleven, ready to burst with impatience, she jumped up and ran down the steps. She would go for a walk, first passing by the garage area, then she would circle the castle, and by the time she returned Michael would have arrived and he'd be waiting for her here, on the steps.

She did—but he wasn't. *Oh, Michael, where are you?* she thought furiously, worriedly, as the sun kept moving inexorably in the sky. Morning died away into afternoon and there was still no sign of her brother.

Around two that afternoon, in a fury at the world but especially at Michael for not having arrived yet and at Carlos for having brought her here in the first place, Anne stormed into the castle and went in search of a telephone. Finding one in a large room that seemed to be a study, she began dialing one number at a time until at last she was answered by a woman's voice; it seemed to be an operator's. Then began what appeared to be a fruitless struggle to make herself understood. She kept insisting that this was an *e–mer–gen–cy*—she did her best to put a Spanish flavor to the word—and finally, after twenty minutes, a woman operator came on the line and asked her in heavily accented English what it was she wanted.

Relieved and grateful, Anne asked to be given the number of Carlos's marine engineering company in Palencia. No, she didn't know the name of the company but there surely couldn't be that many marine engineering companies in one relatively small city, and Carlos's family name, Alvarado-Castellon, had to be well known. Ah, yes, here was a listing, they could put her through.

Once she reached the company, it became another struggle to get to Carlos, but finally his familiar deep voice greeted her courteously on the other end of the wire.

"Carlos," Anne all but screamed at him, her pent-up frustration and rage erupting that moment, "you promised that Michael would be here by last night or this morning! It's midafternoon now and he still isn't here. Did he phone you at all or was that just a lie? If he phoned as you said, why isn't he here? Has he phoned you again? Where is he, Carlos, for heaven's sake!"

"Calm down, Anne," Carlos ordered imperiously. "No, I haven't heard from him again, nor do I have the slightest idea why he has not yet arrived. I'm sorry to hear he's not there and also regret that you're upset, but there is absolutely nothing I can do about either problem and at the moment I'm extremely busy. Please terminate this call and I'll see you tonight. We'll discuss it then."

"Tonight's not good enough!" Anne screamed, and slammed down the phone. She stood for a moment biting her lip, shaking with rage, then swung from the phone and broke into a run out of the study. As she crossed the hall outside she ran across Carlos's father and aunt, regally walking toward the front of the castle. As she hurried by them, she glanced around momentarily and noticed that for the first time the pair of them, startled by her movements, were actually *looking* at her.

"Well, good-bye to you both," Anne threw at them haughtily, the first time she'd addressed either one since that first fearful morning. "I'm packing and leaving this place, which I'm sure you'll both be delighted to hear." By then she was past them, running up the stairs. She did not owe Michael another minute here, and she'd never owed Carlos anything!

As she reached her room upstairs, Anne felt suddenly weak with hunger. Having spent her entire day outside watching for Michael, she'd had nothing whatever to eat. As she opened the heavy door of her room and walked in, she saw with relief that a tray had been left here for her. Bless that sweet old man, she thought, and hurried over to sit down alongside the tray. As she ate, she began to feel a slight bit less frantic. Once she'd finished eating, she would pack and leave, but she no longer felt that leaving had to be accomplished this very minute. She smiled wryly to herself as she realized that once again she was playing a little game with herself. She would pack very carefully, taking her time, and by the time she'd finished, Michael would come bursting through her door. *It's really time you outgrew fairytales,* she cautioned herself, and sipped down the last of her coffee.

She brushed her teeth, combed her hair, and gathered up all her toilet articles. She checked the bathroom with care, checked the bedroom, made one final check to make sure she had absolutely everything, and snapped her case closed. She swung it off the bed, started toward the door, and—just as in her earlier fantasy—the door opened before she could reach it. But it wasn't Michael who came striding in, it was Carlos.

"And where do you think you're going?" Carlos snapped. His face was unnaturally flushed, his breath quick and fast, as though he'd been running. "Father phoned to tell me that you were leaving. Just where do you think you're going?"

Anne stared furiously at Carlos, taking in his handsome, aristocratic face, the sensuous lips that had so often kissed her, the strong supple body against which she had all too frequently pressed. Tears of anger and outrage sprang to her eyes.

"Where I'm going is absolutely no concern of yours!" she cried angrily. "Go to the police, who cares? It was stupid of me ever to listen to you. I never should have come here with you in the first place. Now get out of my way, please. And good-bye!"

Eyes down, face burning with anger, Anne tried to move by him, but Carlos sidestepped to stop her. He grabbed hold of her by one arm, his black eyes sparkling with some emotion she could not fathom.

"But it *is* my concern. I want to know where you're going, and how you plan to get there. We're miles from any city here. Do you think you can walk it? If you leave now, you'll be wandering around in unfamiliar countryside with night only a few hours off. And where will you turn for help, when you can neither speak nor understand Spanish? If you want to leave, all right, tomorrow I'll take you into Palencia with me and see you safely on your way. But not tonight, like this, in this idiotic way. Are you crazy?"

Carlos gave Anne's arm an angry little shake, and she whirled around, unmindful of her tears, to stare him down. His black eyes glittered with a thousand tiny lights and his handsome face looked intently into hers. The next moment he drew Anne against him and his mouth came down on hers, hard, angry, rapacious.

"Tomorrow, Anne," he muttered after the kiss, then again his mouth descended. His arms went around her. He pulled her tightly against him. As his mouth at last released hers, his lips brushed across her cheek, then he kissed her ear, his full mouth warm and frightening. "If you must leave, it can't be until morning," he breathed hotly into her ear, then he swept her up into his arms and carried her over toward the bed. He lowered her onto the bed and fell down upon her in one movement, and Anne couldn't breathe as she felt his weight pin her down, from her ankles to her shoulders.

"Oh, Anne, Anne," Carlos said, his mouth again warm and moist in her ear. He shifted his position to lie beside her and one hand began stroking her arm, then clutched at her waist, then pressed warmly, hungrily, around the curve of her hip, her thigh. Time seemed to stop, become suspended, and Carlos's kisses were lighter one moment, harder the next, one moment hungrily demanding, the next gently, tenderly giving, and all the while his hands roamed her curves and his warm breath caressed her face.

"Oh, Anne, sweetheart, I couldn't let you leave today, like this, without warning," he whispered into her ear. "I was half mad with fear that I might not make it home in time to stop you." Carlos's next kiss was even more passionately demanding than any that had gone before.

How long a time they lay on the bed together kissing, caressing, pressing against each other Anne could never be sure. It seemed very brief; it seemed like forever. Carlos's first kiss was one too many; a million kisses were not enough. Anne wanted to scream out angrily that this hurt too much! She wanted to bury herself against him and plead with him, beg him, never to leave her again. And still he kept kissing her, holding her, caressing every inch of her. Then suddenly his touch grew very light, his lips softened into a gentle tenderness, and to her relief, and distress, he pulled away and stood momentarily by the bed, gazing down at her.

"If you refuse again to come down for dinner, I'll see you in the morning, *mi querida.*" He leaned down for one soft farewell kiss on the cheek, then straightened up, walked to the door and was gone.

Mi querida.

Chapter Twelve

Early the next morning, Anne awakened slowly, aware almost at once that she felt very happy. She lay in bed drowsily enjoying the joyful feeling when suddenly there was a shaft of pain through her joy and she asked herself sharply why she suddenly should feel so pleased with life.

Because today I am leaving here, she told herself. This long, often tedious, bittersweet adventure was drawing to a close and she would once again be free, on her way home. As she lay quietly in bed, fully awake now, she knew that she would often think of these days. The memory of them would never fade, and quite possibly, years from now when she was a white-haired little old lady, she would look back on this time with Carlos as the happiest, most intensely alive period of her life. The pain, the hurt, the loneliness would fade and she'd remember only the marvelous joy and excitement of their day in Paris, the sweet, relaxing, fun-filled days on the Riviera, the all but unbearable intimacy of their night stranded in the mountains in Carlos's car. Even the time spent last evening here on her bed in hungry embrace—the hurt of it would fade while the sweetness of it, the wonder of it, would remain forever, fresh and joyful in memory. Sighing, Anne rolled over onto her side and climbed out of bed.

She was dressing after her shower when a light rap sounded on her door.

"Anne," Carlos called, "may I come in?"

Pulse instantly racing, Anne called back, "Just a moment, please." She hastily tucked her blouse inside the waistband of her suit skirt, zipped up the side, and called, "All right, Carlos, come on in."

The door opened and he stood on the threshold, superbly dressed in casual yet elegant sports clothes that emphasized his lean, totally masculine build. As always, she was struck by how incredibly handsome he was, his aristocratic face, framed by the thick, shining black hair, so very dear to her now. His black eyes, shadowed-looking, gazed back at her with a question in their depths.

"Do you still plan to leave today?" Carlos asked.

"Of course!" Anne replied with a touch of tartness, pulse racing even faster.

Carlos eyed her a moment longer, then sighed. "Well, if you must, I'll delay going in to the office and drive you to the city to arrange for your transportation. But for now, Anne, please do come downstairs to join us for breakfast."

"Who is 'us'?" Anne asked, instantly wary.

Carlos looked startled. "Why, my father, aunt, and myself, of course."

"And Maria?"

"Maria left here two days ago. I assumed you knew. We'll wait for you to join us downstairs." With that, he turned on his heel and closed the door.

A few minutes later Anne walked tensely down the stairs toward the dining room. She had no wish to face the elderly duke and his sister again but felt she had very little choice. The last thing she wanted to do now was offend Carlos, alienate him so that he changed his mind about taking her into Palencia and arranging her transportation. And one way or another she would survive breakfast with the arrogantly noble trio, she felt sure.

As she entered the dining room, Carlos, who stood by the sideboard pouring a cup of coffee, glanced around at once and smiled at her. His father, who sat at the table, glanced around too and immediately rose to his feet. *Courteous at all costs*, Anne thought, her lips twitching wryly; arrogant, cold, snobbish, but nevertheless forever courteous. With a slight, nervous smile she bowed her head to the duke and he bowed stiffly back and reseated himself. Carlos's Aunt Isabel gazed directly at Anne as she walked in but acknowledged her arrival only with a coldly self-righteous, twitching little smile.

As the elderly valet brought hot serving dishes to the table and served everyone, no word was said. Anne, whose initial discomfort had been acute, began to feel almost relaxed. Neither the duke nor his sister seemed inclined to address her or berate her, thank heavens. They seemed content simply to ignore her presence, which was fine. The food was, as always, mouthwateringly good, and an ample breakfast would stand her in good stead for her travels ahead. She found, happily enough, that she was able to ignore the company in which she found herself and enjoy her meal quite as much as if she were upstairs in her room alone. She ate with hearty appetite, and felt renewed.

She was still enjoying her last cup of coffee when Carlos's aunt rose and with an arrogant sniff excused herself, glancing at Anne with an aggrieved expression as much as to say that her unwanted presence had spoiled the meal for her. As his sister left, the elderly duke rose and excused himself too. Left alone with Carlos, Anne felt suddenly rather embarrassed. She gulped down what was left of her coffee and rose to leave as well.

"Why the sudden rush?" Carlos asked. "It's still very early and we have plenty of time. Would you mind sitting down for a moment so that I might talk with you?"

Anne did as he requested, feeling suddenly breathless. Her eyes met his. "About what?"

Carlos's black eyes stayed on hers for several moments, then with a little sigh he glanced away. "I'm sorry," he murmured. "I feel as though there is so much I wish to discuss with you, but when the opportunity presents itself, I—how do you Americans put it?—I draw a blank." His eyes returned to hers and he smiled, a bemused, half-regretful smile such as Anne had never seen on his lips before. One hand lay on the table top and Anne noticed in surprise, as her eyes lowered, that the hand was drawn into a fist.

He sighed deeply again. "Well, never mind. Once you have left, once you are actually gone, I know I shall curse at myself for not having spoken out, for remaining silent. We come from such different worlds"—as he said this, Carlos's eyes again met

175

Anne's, and he looked at her with what seemed like infinite sadness in the black depths of those eyes—"do we not, *mi querida?*" His voice was so soft as he said this that Anne, though she sat only a few feet away, had to strain to hear.

"Yes, Carlos, we do," Anne agreed, unwelcome tears coming into her eyes. "Yet at moments, at certain moments—"

"Yes?"

Anne shook her head nervously, glancing away. "Well, never mind, I have drawn a blank too. I just want you to know, Carlos, that—well, that"—she glanced back, daring to meet those black eyes again —"that at certain moments I've felt extremely close to you, and that no matter how long I live, or who I marry, there will always be a special place in my heart reserved for you. I know so well that I'll never forget you."

"Nor I you." Carlos reached out to press his hand over Anne's, still smiling the same bemused smile. "And now I suppose you'd better go up to finish packing before we depart."

"Yes, I suppose."

After she rose, Anne stepped over to Carlos's side, leaned down and pressed a kiss on his cheek. "In many ways I'm grateful to you, Carlos, and in many ways I—" She couldn't complete the sentence, say the words "I love you." Straightening up quickly, she hurried out of the room, not once glancing back.

She was descending the stairs a brief time later, carrying her one case, when the front door was thrown open and Dorrie walked in, followed by

Michael. The sight of the two of them so startled Anne that she dropped her case and stopped walking, frozen to her spot on the stairs. Not only Michael, Dorrie too! The prodigals had returned.

Carlos was walking down the hall toward the front entry and saw the young couple almost at the same instant that Anne did.

"Dolores! I can't believe it!" In a few long strides he reached his sister's side, grabbing hold of her by the shoulders. "Dolores, are you well? Are you home for good? Father will be so happy to see you! And this is Michael, I presume?"

As Carlos turned to face Michael, his handsome face hardened, his expression becoming impassive, and Anne thought for a moment that he was going to refuse to shake the hand that Michael nervously extended. But good manners prevailed, and Carlos put his own hand out to momentarily shake the one offered to him.

"I was just preparing to drive your sister into the city," Carlos told Michael, cool arrogance in his voice. "She had despaired of your keeping your word and returning as you had promised to do."

By then Anne had picked up her case again and descended the last few stairs. Michael's green eyes swung around to gaze beseechingly at her.

"Anne, I'm so dreadfully sorry." As he stood gazing at her, blinking nervously, he looked and sounded extremely fatigued. "I told Dorrie a hundred times I was coming here no matter what, but she found a thousand ways to delay me. It's been a constant, never-ending battle, which doesn't excuse me, I know. I'm sure you must be terribly angry at

177

me now, but I only hope that someday you'll get over your anger and forgive me. It's been such a frightful mess."

Suddenly, to Anne's eyes, Michael looked about five years old, a brave little boy doing his best not to cry. As he hung his head, she rushed to him, gave him a hug, and assured him she was no longer the least bit angry.

"It's just that I was so terribly worried," she told him, forgetting for the moment that she'd ever felt any anger. "And now that you're here, I'm so relieved. But, Dorrie, how are you? It's wonderful to see you too," Anne added, swinging to face the girl Michael loved, extending her hand as she smiled.

Dorrie thrust her chin a little higher into the air and for a moment angrily ignored Anne's extended hand. But then, as with her brother, training prevailed and she resentfully put her own hand out, slipping her slim, smooth palm into Anne's.

"I'm well enough," she answered coolly, "considering that I gave my heart to a man who soon proved that he felt no love for me at all. It seems that everyone else in the world matters more to him than I do."

"Dorrie, that's not true," Michael protested, his eyes fastening beseechingly on Dorrie's pale face. "You know I love you, that I'm so crazy about you—"

"Crazy, yes!" Dorrie snapped back, blinking against the sudden tears that had appeared in her eyes. "But actions speak louder than words, you know, and your actions prove what a liar you are! If you loved me we'd be in America now, we'd be married! We wouldn't be here where my father and brother can lock me up and make me their prisoner!"

In a fury Dorrie swung around and stepped toward her brother. "Here, jailor," she cried, grabbing a package out of her coat pocket and slapping it into Carlos's hands, "here are the jewels you said we stole. Now you've got what you want, Michael's got what he wants, Anne's got what she wants, everybody's got what he wants except for me!"

Saying this, Dorrie broke into tears. Dropping her face into her hands, she cried heartbrokenly, shaking with her sobs. When Carlos, looking stricken, stepped forward and tried to comfort her, she pulled angrily away. Michael, who put his arm around her, murmuring soothing words, fared no better.

"Just leave me alone, both of you, just leave me alone!" Crying, she hurried across the vast entry hall and began running up the stairs. Three pairs of eyes watched her departure, but no word was said. Only after Dorrie had disappeared down the upstairs hall did Carlos speak.

"Excuse me, please. I must go find my father and aunt to let them know that Dolores is home."

Anne and Michael sat out on the front steps, on the warm stone, quietly discussing everything that had happened. Around eleven Carlos stepped out through the heavy carved door and asked them courteously if they would please come inside.

"We're having a family conference in the sitting room," he explained, "and Dolores insists that Michael be there."

Anne rose nervously, feeling a bit unsteady. "And —you want me there too?"

"Yes, Anne, please, if you wouldn't mind."

The sitting room was very large, decorated in muted tones, a room heavy with tradition and repressive breeding, a room where loud voices and shrill argument had no place. But there's a first time for everything, Anne thought wryly, as she and Michael followed Carlos inside.

The elderly duke stood by a huge, open-hearth fireplace, his gray-streaked, immaculately trimmed Vandyke beard giving his stern face an even sterner look. He stood magnificently erect, as always, gazing across at them with arrogant impassivity. His tall white-haired sister sat at one end of a brocaded sofa, her dark eyes gazing regally right through them. Dorrie stood within a few feet of her father, her carriage as erect as his, her head thrown back, firm chin thrust defiantly into the air. With a quick, unexpected spurt of amusement it occurred to Anne that Dolores, for all her youth, would possibly prove to be a match for both her father and brother, even with her aunt thrown in. There was something so stubbornly self-assured, so stubbornly willful, about her slim young body, her lovely young face, it was hard to believe that she couldn't wrestle from life absolutely anything she wanted. But apparently, Anne thought with a sigh, she no longer wanted Michael. Or—did she?

Carlos walked over to stand near his father and quietly took charge.

"Anne, Michael, we've asked you to join us here as father wishes to discuss what actions we ought to take against Michael for my sister's lengthy absence." Dorrie here interrupted with a loud, contemptuous snort, which Carlos ignored. His voice stayed even, calm, and cool. "My own feelings are we should simply forget this unfortunate affair ever took place. My father, however—"

"—stupidly insists that Michael should be arrested and thrown into jail," Dorrie threw in.

Carlos's head whipped around as he glared at his sister. "Dolores, watch your tongue," he commanded. "It is insufferable that you should speak to or about your father in such a way."

Dorrie's eyes glared back at her brother with equal anger. Instead of flinching, she thrust her chin even higher into the air. "Well, when he insists upon something so stupid, so utterly stupid—"

"Dolores, I'm warning you—"

"One more word out of you, young lady, and I'll have you sent to your room and locked up again," the elderly duke announced, gleaming dark eyes fastening coldly on his daughter.

"For how long?" Dorrie cried, challenging her father.

"For as long as it takes to teach you proper respect!" her father snapped.

"The rest of my life, you mean? Well, just remember what happened the last time you tried that—I managed to get away, didn't I? And I will again. This isn't the Middle Ages, you know. You can't just put people under lock and key and keep them prisoners forever. I'll find some way to get word out to Michael, as I did last time, and off we'll go again, only next time we'll get married at once and then you'll never be able to drag me back. *Never!*" Dorrie glared triumphantly at her father.

Her aunt broke in, pouring out a torrent of words in Spanish that Anne, of course, couldn't understand. To her surprise Michael responded to Aunt Isabel, also speaking in Spanish—apparently Dorrie had taught him more than how to get involved in a miserably mixed-up love affair. Carlos spoke angrily to Michael, the elderly duke had his say, Aunt Isabel spoke again, Dorrie argued wildly, angrily, gesticulating—all of them speaking in Spanish. The angry confrontation grew even louder, with shrill voices breaking in, interrupting, overriding, trying to silence the opposition. As the noise swirled around her, streams of angry argument that she could not begin to follow, Anne realized suddenly that she had a terrible headache. Everyone was ignoring her and she could not possibly contribute anything to the discussion as she hadn't the least idea who was arguing what. Abruptly she felt too frustrated, too incensed, to be a mute witness any longer. Let them rant and rave all they liked, but without her. She swung around and walked hurriedly out of the room, instinctively holding her breath until she reached the hall and could relax and breathe again. She'd go outside, into the lovely quiet garden, and wait out the storm.

She had just stepped onto the graveled path of the front rose garden when she heard a rapid stride following her. She glanced around and saw in surprise that it was Carlos, his handsome face shadowed. He approached to within a few feet of her, then stopped and stared insistently at her, his black eyes grave.

"Why did you run out just now? Have you no interest in your brother's fate?" As Anne started to protest that of course she did, she saw the incipient twinkle in Carlos's dark eyes. "Or were you perfectly sure that this was another argument full of sound and fury, signifying nothing?"

Anne felt her lips twitch into an amused little smile. "Well, yes, I suppose I felt reasonably certain that now that you have both your sister and the jewelry back, there'd be no particular purpose in charging my brother with a crime you've already agreed he didn't commit. In that sense, Dorrie was surely right that any other course was rather, if you'll excuse the word, stupid." Anne paused momentarily, her smile dying away. "How soon do you suppose the confrontation will end and we can be on our way?"

The suggestion of an amused smile on Carlos's lips instantly died away. An oddly intense look came over his face, a look that frightened her a little. As warm as it was in the late-morning sun, she felt herself shiver slightly. Instead of answering her question, Carlos stepped toward her.

"Despite her youth and willfulness, Dolores was right about other things too." Carlos spoke in an oddly tense voice. "I've only just realized this. When she found a man she loved, a man who gave great joy and meaning to her life, she didn't try to fight it, to reason it away. From the very night we met I knew how I felt about you, that I enjoyed looking at you, being with you, as I've never enjoyed being with any woman before. I couldn't bear the thought of having you leave, yet still I was going to let you go, even help you to go, without telling you how I felt, without admitting how much I love you and asking whether you would possibly do me the honor of being my wife. Will you, Anne?"

Momentarily Anne felt too stunned to answer, then with an irrepressible smile she moved forward and the next moment she was joyfully in Carlos's arms. "Oh, Carlos, yes. I love you too."

"As my sister loves your brother, that is how I love you," Carlos murmured, then pressed his soft, full mouth tenderly down on hers.

After the kiss ended, Anne inquired curiously, "Then you think Dorrie still loves my brother, in spite of what she has said?"

Carlos, drawing Anne even closer, burst out with a brief, happy laugh. "But of course. Can feeling a little anger at someone, even a great deal of anger, kill off love? You saw how she was, ready to battle our father, our aunt, me, battle the world to save Michael trouble. Isn't that proof of love?"

"Well, I suppose," Anne murmured, laughing too.

A minute later she and Carlos started back toward the castle, his arm around her, while Anne gazed with utter contentment into the wonderfully handsome face she so loved. "Do you think there's any chance that your father will withdraw his objections and allow them to marry? And, oh dear, what about us?" Anne stopped walking. "Won't he object strongly to me? And—what about Maria? Oh, Carlos, are you sure you meant what you just said?"

Carlos stopped walking, swung to face Anne, and gently pushed a lock of golden brown hair away from her brow. "With my entire heart and soul I meant it," he said softly. "About Maria, I told you before we were never formally engaged, it was just an understanding. She'll have no choice but to adjust, to realize that I've reached a new understanding—of myself, of my heart—with someone else. As for my father"—Carlos shrugged lightly, smiling—"well, I'd be lying if I told you he will be pleased. He won't be. Neither will my aunt. They are old, as you've seen, and set in their ways. But while I owe them both respect and love, I don't owe them my life. I'm free to marry whomever I please. And with your permission, I am most wonderfully pleased to marry you."

Carlos kissed her with greater tenderness, with greater love, than ever before.

"And—Michael and your sister?" Anne asked a moment later as they walked on again.

Carlos grinned. "Oh, Dorrie will get her Michael, don't worry about that. When I take my sister's side and urge father to consent, he won't be happy about it but he'll be forced to give in. What else can he do? As Dolores reminded him so rudely just now, we no longer live in the Middle Ages. This is twentieth-century Spain, and we shall all marry our heart's desire and live happily ever after." Carlos stopped walking, caught hold of Anne by the shoulders, and his black eyes gazed intently down into hers. "Won't we, my love?"

He did not wait for her answer, but leaned quickly, urgently down to kiss her, while Anne's heart raced and she told herself that surely, surely, it was so—they *would* live happily ever after. With a soft, happy little sigh she slipped her arms around Carlos's neck as he held her close against him for a solemn betrothal kiss.

Silhouette 🖤 *Romance*

15-Day Free Trial Offer
6 Silhouette Romances

6 Silhouette Romances, free for 15 days! We'll send you 6 new Silhouette Romances to keep for 15 days, absolutely free! If you decide not to keep them, send them back to us. You pay nothing.

Free Home Delivery. But if you enjoy them as much as we think you will, keep them by paying the invoice enclosed with your free trial shipment. We'll pay all shipping and handling charges. You get the convenience of Home Delivery and we pay the postage and handling charge each month.

Don't miss a copy. The Silhouette Book Club is the way to make sure you'll be able to receive every new romance we publish before they're sold out. There is no minimum number of books to buy and you can cancel at any time.

Silhouette ❤ *Romance*

IT'S YOUR OWN SPECIAL TIME

Contemporary romances for today's women.
Each month, six very special love stories will be yours
from SILHOUETTE. Look for them wherever books are sold
or order now from the coupon below.

$1.50 each

Hampson	☐ 1	☐ 4	☐ 16	☐ 27	Browning	☐ 12	☐ 38	☐ 53	☐ 73
	☐ 28	☐ 40	☐ 52	☐ 64	☐ 94		☐ 93		
Stanford	☐ 6	☐ 25	☐ 35	☐ 46	Michaels	☐ 15	☐ 32	☐ 61	☐ 87
	☐ 58	☐ 88			John	☐ 17	☐ 34	☐ 57	☐ 85
Hastings	☐ 13	☐ 26	☐ 44	☐ 67	Beckman	☐ 8	☐ 37	☐ 54	☐ 72
Vitek	☐ 33	☐ 47	☐ 66	☐ 84		☐ 96			

$1.50 each

☐ 5 Goforth	☐ 29 Wildman	☐ 56 Trent	☐ 79 Halldorson
☐ 7 Lewis	☐ 30 Dixon	☐ 59 Vernon	☐ 80 Stephens
☐ 9 Wilson	☐ 31 Halldorson	☐ 60 Hill	☐ 81 Roberts
☐ 10 Caine	☐ 36 McKay	☐ 62 Hallston	☐ 82 Dailey
☐ 11 Vernon	☐ 39 Sinclair	☐ 63 Brent	☐ 83 Hallston
☐ 14 Oliver	☐ 41 Owen	☐ 69 St. George	☐ 86 Adams
☐ 19 Thornton	☐ 42 Powers	☐ 70 Afton Bonds	☐ 89 James
☐ 20 Fulford	☐ 43 Robb	☐ 71 Ripy	☐ 90 Major
☐ 21 Richards	☐ 45 Carroll	☐ 74 Trent	☐ 92 McKay
☐ 22 Stephens	☐ 48 Wildman	☐ 75 Carroll	☐ 95 Wisdom
☐ 23 Edwards	☐ 49 Wisdom	☐ 76 Hardy	☐ 97 Clay
☐ 24 Healy	☐ 50 Scott	☐ 77 Cork	☐ 98 St. George
	☐ 55 Ladame	☐ 78 Oliver	☐ 99 Camp

$1.75 each

☐ 100 Stanford	☐ 105 Eden	☐ 110 Trent	☐ 115 John
☐ 101 Hardy	☐ 106 Dalley	☐ 111 South	☐ 116 Lindley
☐ 102 Hastings	☐ 107 Bright	☐ 112 Stanford	☐ 117 Scott
☐ 103 Cork	☐ 108 Hampson	☐ 113 Browning	☐ 118 Dailey
☐ 104 Vitek	☐ 109 Vernon	☐ 114 Michaels	☐ 119 Hampson

6 brand new
Silhouette Special Editions
yours for 15 days–Free!

For the reader who wants more...more story...more detail and description...more realism...and more romance...in paperback originals, 1/3 longer than our regular Silhouette Romances. Love lingers longer in new Silhouette Special Editions. Love weaves an intricate, provocative path in a third more pages than you have just enjoyed. It is love as you have always wanted it to be—and more —intriguingly depicted by your favorite Silhouette authors in the inimitable Silhouette style.

15-Day Free Trial Offer

We will send you 6 new Silhouette Special Editions to keep for 15 days absolutely free! If you decide not to keep them, send them back to us, you pay nothing. But if you enjoy them as much as we think you will, keep them and pay the invoice enclosed with your trial shipment. You will then automatically become a member of the Special Edition Book Club and receive 6 more romances every month. There is no minimum number of books to buy and you can cancel at any time.

Available in June.

Silhouette Romance

Coming next month from
Silhouette Romances

Reluctant Deceiver by Dorothy Cork

When Merlyn flew to Hong Kong under false pretenses, her plan backfired. Sullivan, the only man she would ever love, refused to believe in her innocence.

The Kissing Time by Jean Saunders

When Julie is hired as Vince's research assistant, she learns that when the gorse is in bloom on the Scottish tundra, it is indeed, "the kissing time."

A Touch Of Fire by Ann Major

When Helen Freeman books a room in a Paris hotel she finds that a handsome stranger has prior claim to it and he intends to take full advantage of their impromptu introduction.

A Kiss And A Promise by Anne Hampson

After Judith broke her engagement with Alexis she thought their love had died. But when she went to live in his house as a nanny to his young nephew, she discovered that love can be rekindled.

Undercover Girl by Carole Halston

Reporter Kelly Lindsay was thrilled at the prospect of living undercover in Palm Beach. But she had never imagined that she would fall in love with the subject of her exposé!

Wildcatter's Woman by Janet Dailey

After years of divorce, Veronica realized that Race was the same irresponsible wildcatter she'd walked out on—but he also hadn't lost his heart-stoppingly powerful, sensual magnetism.

**Look for *Daring Encounter* by Patti Beckman
Available in June.**

READERS' COMMENTS ON SILHOUETTE ROMANCES:

"I would like to congratulate you on the most wonderful books I've had the pleasure of reading. They are a tremendous joy to those of us who have yet to meet the man of our dreams. From reading your books I quite truly believe that he will some-day appear before me like a prince!"

—L.L.*, Hollandale, MS

"Your books are great, wholesome fiction, always with an upbeat, happy ending. Thank you."

—M.D., Massena, NY

"My boyfriend always teases me about Silhouette Books. He asks me, how's my love life and natu-rally I say terrific, but I tell him that there is always room for a little more romance from Sil-houette."

—F.N., Ontario, Canada

"I would like to sincerely express my gratitude to you and your staff for bringing the pleasure of your publications to my attention. Your books are well written, mature and very contemporary."

—D.D., Staten Island, NY

*names available on request